"I literally could not stop reading this book. I ignored
my children as they pleaded with me to serve them
food and beverages. I ignored my weenie dog
who was whining to go outside to do her business.
I refused to do the laundry, pay the bills, or answer
the phone. I inhaled this book from cover to cover."
—*Penelope's Romance Reviews*

"4½ stars. [A] spectacular Blaze debut."
—*RT Book Reviews*

"Ms. Maguire can sure write a kick-ass love scene."
—*Cheeky Reads*

"I loved this story and instantly fell in love
with both characters."
—*Night Owl Reviews*

Blaze

Dear Reader,

We have exciting news! As I'm sure you've noticed, the Harlequin Blaze books you know and love have a brand-new look, starting this month. And it's *hot!* Don't you agree?

But don't worry—nothing else about the Blaze books has changed. You'll still find those unforgettable love stories with intrepid heroines, hot, hunky heroes and a double dose of sizzle!

Check out this month's red-hot reads....

#729 THE RISK-TAKER by Kira Sinclair
(Uniformly Hot!)

#730 LYING IN BED by Jo Leigh
(The Wrong Bed)

#731 HIS KIND OF TROUBLE by Samantha Hunter
(The Berringers)

#732 ONE MORE KISS by Kathy Garbera

#733 RELENTLESS SEDUCTION by Jillian Burns

#734 THE WEDDING FLING by Meg Maguire

I hope you're as pleased with our new look as we are. Drop by www.Harlequin.com or www.blazeauthors.com to let us know what you think.

Brenda Chin
Senior Editor
Harlequin Blaze

The Wedding Fling

Meg Maguire

HARLEQUIN®
entertain, enrich, inspire™

Recycling programs
for this product may
not exist in your area.

ISBN-13: 978-0-373-79738-7

THE WEDDING FLING

Copyright © 2013 by Meg Maguire

ABOUT THE AUTHOR

Before becoming a writer, Meg Maguire worked as a record store snob, a lousy barista, a decent designer and an overenthusiastic penguin handler. Now she loves writing sexy, character-driven stories about strong-willed men and women who keep each other on their toes...and bring one another to their knees. Meg lives north of Boston with her husband. When she's not trapped in her own head she can be found in the kitchen, the coffee shop or jogging around the nearest duck-filled pond.

Books by Meg Maguire

HARLEQUIN BLAZE
608—CAUGHT ON CAMERA

To get the inside scoop on Harlequin Blaze and its talented writers, be sure to check out blazeauthors.com.

Other titles by this author available in ebook format. Don't miss any of our special offers. Write to us at the following address for information on our newest releases.

Harlequin Reader Service
U.S.: 3010 Walden Ave., P.O. Box 1325, Buffalo, NY 14269
Canadian: P.O. Box 609, Fort Erie, Ont. L2A 5X3

With thanks to Amy, Ruthie and Serena,
for reading it first. Thanks also to Laura
for getting me on the plane, and to Brenda for
landing us with minimal turbulence. Biggest thanks
of all to my husband, bringer of peanut butter.

1

LEIGH MADE A NEST in the rumpled sheets of her hotel room bed, arranging a napkin, spoon and peanut butter jar before her. She unscrewed the lid and set it aside, plunging the spoon deep to coat its back. As she savored the first taste, her anxiety dulled, worries temporarily forgotten.

She looked at the television, where two nattering entertainment anchors discussed the latest Hollywood wedding.

"The big question, of course, is the dress. After that taffeta fiasco at the Golden Globes, I know we're all holding our breath."

The anchors disappeared, replaced by a still of the sequined dress in question. Leigh frowned. She liked that dress. She jabbed her spoon back into the jar, barely tasting the next hundred calories' worth of comfort as she licked it clean.

"Then again, that Grammy dress was a solid A," one host said.

"Absolutely," his perky colleague agreed. *"When she gets it right, she nails it."*

Leigh watched the footage of the demure young woman on the red carpet pausing for photos, looking so calm and happy. Makeup flawless, styled hair bouncing, golden highlights glinting with each camera flash. Must be nice to be the girl on TV.

Stretching her legs in front of her, Leigh wondered what the media would make of her pajamas' holly-and-ivy pattern in April. Then she looked to the jar in her hand and realized she probably had worse faux pas to worry about.

"Now, Leigh Bailey might be Hollywood's last good girl, but what do we think? White dress?"

Simpering laughter. *"She may be scandal-proof, but she* is *marrying a musician, let's not forget that."*

Across the room, Leigh's phone chimed, her mom's ring tone triggering a fresh stab of panic that broke the peanut butter's spell. She scrambled from the tangle of covers, gooey spoon landing on the white duvet. "Crap." But this was L.A. The housekeeping staff had surely seen far worse.

She padded to the bureau and hit Talk. "Hi, Ma."

"Leigh, where are you?"

"I'm eating peanut butter in bed, watching tabloid shows."

"Honey." A sigh, equal parts fond and frustrated; her mother to a tee. "The fitter's already here in the suite. It's nine-thirty."

"I know what time it is."

"And she's the best in town, but you shouldn't eat that garbage hours before you're going to be seen in a fitted satin sheath by half the city. People will say you're pregnant."

It was Leigh's turn to sigh. She turned to the TV in time to catch footage of herself in a bikini.

"Those shots from Maui," the anchor was saying.

"She's never looked better," his partner concurred.

Leigh smiled drily. Lovely. Two weeks with the violent stomach bug that exiled her to the bathroom for most of her vacation…but she'd never looked better! She glanced longingly at the jar on her bed.

"Leigh?"

"Yeah?"

"When, honey?"

"I need to shower. Twenty minutes?"

"Twenty minutes, but *twenty minutes*. Not thirty, not an hour. We need the fitting done by eleven, before the makeup and hair people arrive. Then the photographers—"

"I'll be there."

"This isn't some premiere, Leigh Bailey. It's your wedding day." Ah, the patented maternal use of the full name. The big guns were coming out.

"The day I should be in flip-flops and a sundress, in Grandma's backyard," Leigh said, frustration making her sound bitter. Making her sound distinctly like her mother. "I wanted a barbecue. I wanted you and Dad and Cody there, and Dan's family. I didn't want eight hundred people I barely even know, at some gigantic estate." Funny how the guests had multiplied, the locale shifted and the budget exploded as Leigh's day had morphed from a cookout to a circus, in six months flat.

The ringmaster went on. "It doesn't work that way when you're a star, honey."

"I'm not a star, Ma. I'm just some girl who's always in the magazines. I haven't been in a movie in two years."

"That's not what it's about these days. What channel are you watching?"

"Fifty-one."

"Us, too. And who's the main story?"

"Me." Glancing again to the bedspread, she wondered idly if it was possible to OD on peanut butter. She imagined a team of burly EMTs crashing through the door to find her slumped with a spoon dangling from her mouth, TV droning, bed and carpet littered with empty jars.

"Following an apparent cry-for-help binge, Leigh Bailey was found unconscious the morning of her wedding from an

*alleged peanut butter overdose. Doctors administered grape
jelly intravenously, and the actress is now listed in stable condition. The wedding has been postponed until further notice."*

Her mother burst through the daydream. "Leigh?"

"Sorry, what?"

"I said you *are* a star, honey. And I know you wanted to
keep things simple, but think about Dan. Dan wants all this."

"He didn't before." A queasy gurgle soured Leigh's stomach. Dan *did* want all this, the circus. She sometimes wondered which woman her fiancé saw her as—the one on TV
having her clothes and waistline critiqued, or the one in her
pj's. Dan used to be her anchor, keeping her grounded amid
the chaos, but small changes over two years had added up. A
new apartment, wardrobe, a new collection of opinions about
which restaurants they could or couldn't go to. Just like the
mutant wedding, their relationship had changed, its modifi-
cations too incremental to spot without hindsight.

Dan used to talk about his music, where the band was
going. The band hadn't practiced in months, and his enthusiasm for songwriting had been replaced with talk of producing,
investing in a label, opening a club. More driven by cachet
than creativity. Sometimes Leigh worried he'd bought in to
the myth of that girl on the screen. Sometimes she bought in
to it herself, though not lately. Not since the impending wedding had grown to such epic proportions.

"Do you think he still loves me?" Leigh asked her mother.

"Of course Dan loves you. You two are perfect together."

As if on cue, footage of her and Dan from early in their
coupledom appeared on the TV. She really did look happy.
She looked like herself, recognizable, Dan so at ease in his
own scruffy skin, back when he'd been a happy and passionate nobody. She hadn't seen him smile at her that way
in months. He smiled *through* her these days, like a man focused on something beyond his grasp, something behind her.

"Every bride gets wedding-day jitters. If you didn't feel nervous, we'd have something to worry about." There was jingling behind her mom's words, the sound of jewelry being adjusted.

"Right."

"Now get in that shower, young lady."

They hung up and Leigh shuffled to her suite's gorgeous bathroom, all polished marble and glass. After a shampoo and scrub, she slicked lotion on her waxed legs, toweled her hair and brushed her teeth, so freshly bleached they ached. "You, only *better*," as her mother said of such enhancements. But weren't moms supposed to love you exactly the way you were?

Leigh wiped the steam from the mirror and stared at her naked reflection, glad she'd never let herself be talked into changing anything major—bigger boobs would look ridiculous on her frame, and would be a liability if she ever started dancing again. She was already admired for her pale, creamy complexion, so tanning was mercifully off the table. She looked at her nails, shaped and buffed by a manicurist, but fundamentally hers.

Her engagement ring sparkled under the bulbs circling the mirror. So pretty. And she'd fought so hard to keep it, against her mother's protests that it was too small, too simple, too *anybody's*. But like the boobs, Leigh thought small-and-understated suited her fine. She polished the solitaire with a tissue, feeling better as she dressed to face the drama surely swirling in her mother's suite. The bridal suite, sans bride.

She walked down the long hall to the opposite corner of the hotel's twenty-first floor and knocked. Her mother answered at once, already styled, as though a wedding were a tornado that might touch down at any moment and must be vigilantly prepared for. She had her cell clamped to her ear, and her tone made Leigh's chest tighten. It could only be her father on the other end.

"You *are* kidding me. Jesus, Jim. It's like you get off on not listening to— No, I never said that. Not only do you not listen, you just make up whatever it is you want me to be saying." She glanced at Leigh. "Your daughter is here. The one who's getting married, or will be if you can manage to get your act together. Right. We'll talk about this later."

Unseen, Leigh rolled her eyes. *No, you won't.* They'd *fight* later, turning yet another non-issue into a marriage referendum as they'd been doing for as long as Leigh could remember. All those years ago she'd thrown herself into dancing, ballet at first, then modern, any and all kinds, whatever got her out of the house and the endless two-way badgering. When she'd landed her first movie role her parents had magically stopped bickering, united in their new project—Leigh's career. Of course, the peace hadn't lasted, but here she was ten years later, still desperate to be the good girl, successful and respectable, her naive inner kid thinking she could somehow fix them, if only she worked hard enough.

Her mom clicked the phone off and shook her head, her frosted bob too shellacked with products to budge. She sighed in exasperation, then changed modes, quick as a flipped switch. She smiled warmly and pulled Leigh into a hug. "Oh, honey. Your big day." She stepped back to stare at her daughter's face. "It's finally here, isn't it?"

Leigh nodded, returning her mom's grin as best she could.

"Twenty-seven. When on earth did that happen?"

When, indeed. And twenty-seven was far too old to still be living for parental approval. Leigh pictured the plane ticket in her purse. When she landed back in the States in a couple weeks, she'd put her foot down. Her parents had their own lives to lead, and so did Leigh. If only she knew what she wanted that life to look like...

Her mother turned to the action elsewhere in the room, the

wedding planner on his phone, the fitter standing patiently beside the ivory halter gown.

That dress. The battle Leigh had forfeited in favor of winning the war on her ring. The ring she'd wear for the rest of her life, the gown just a day. But it was a lovely dress. More sophisticated than the playful one Leigh had fallen hard for, but compromises had to be made to keep mothers happy... or at least shut them up.

"Beautiful, isn't it?" her mom said.

"Yeah, it is."

"Glad you let me talk you into it now? It's just perfect for the venue."

Leigh nodded, so sick of certain words—*venue, entrance, presentation.*

She let herself be led to the fitter and dutifully stripped. The dress was slippery and cool as lake water as it slid down her bare skin, and she felt clad in something beyond satin... adulthood, perhaps. Womanhood. Her mother tugged her from the thought.

"Oh, Leigh." She tapped a finger against Leigh's belly. And only in L.A. would it count as a belly. "You and that peanut butter."

Leigh smoothed the satin over her offense. "Girls should know it's normal to have a stomach."

"I agree, but it's *not* normal for a person to eat half a jar of that stuff by herself. It's very fattening, and you won't have that metabolism forever."

Leigh shrugged. "Tell me you'd prefer I take up smoking, then."

Her pack-a-day mother smiled grimly and dropped the subject. "Well, you look beautiful, belly and all."

Leigh turned to the cheval mirror at her side, and she had to admit the girl reflected back was pretty. Though once her hair and makeup were done, her snack digested and belly deflated, would there be anything of Leigh left?

She looked to her mom. "Do you remember what you promised me? My wedding gift? About quitting smoking once all this craziness is over?"

"I remember."

Leigh grinned hopefully. "So I'll get back from the island and you'll be all strung out and snappy?"

"I'll do better than that, honey, and finish the withdrawal while you're away."

Leigh smiled again. Though her mother promised to quit smoking nearly as often as she lit up. "There's other stuff that needs to change, once I'm back."

Her mother feigned ignorance, fussing with some invisible imperfection in the satin. "Oh?"

"About you and Dad? Maybe going on a trip of your own, away from all this?"

"I don't know, Leigh. I've got a hundred things going on, all that stuff with the charity ball coming up in June."

Leigh opened her mouth, then closed it, realizing she didn't have the stamina for this argument. But once she got back from her honeymoon she'd be putting her own marriage first, instead of acting like a smoke screen in theirs. Once today was behind her, she'd be in the clear. Marriage would render her blissfully boring to the press, and she couldn't wait to fade into obscurity for a year or two, maybe permanently. Fame had never been her dream. Just another role she'd stumbled into, trying to make people happy.

She stared out the huge window across the city. What would Dan be doing, right now? Probably sleeping in, after his bachelor party. Not that Dan was much for getting wasted and crazy. He was a pretty low-key guy. Or he used to be a pretty low-key guy. Who he was wasn't so clear anymore.

She missed his passion. Their hectic, high-profile engagement had done a number on their sex life, and Leigh suspected he was readjusting how he saw her, no longer his girlfriend, but his soon-to-be wife.

When the fitter got to her knees to fuss with the hem, Leigh leaned close to her mother's ear to whisper, "I don't think Dan and I have had sex in nearly a month."

"You're very busy people."

"No one's *that* busy. We're not even newlyweds yet. That can't be normal, can it?"

"You and Dan aren't normal people. And Dan is very ambitious. You're lucky to have such a driven man, Leigh, really. Not like your father—"

"Ma."

"A lot of girls in your position have husbands who don't expect to do a thing after they get a nice tight grip on those celebrity coattails. Dan's not one of them. You're very, very lucky."

Leigh knew she ought to feel lucky. The man she was marrying was her best friend. Or had been. She prayed they'd get some of that back, being away from everyone for two weeks. No, they *would* get it back. She needed to think positive. Still, a bit of reassurance wouldn't hurt.

When the fitter excused herself to make a call, Leigh thought she ought to do the same. She padded back down the hall to her own room, shut the door and stood before the windows, holding down a button on her phone to speed-dial Dan.

He answered just as she was about to hang up, and his voice alone reminded her to breathe. "Hey, you. What's up?"

"Hey. I, um… Oh God, I don't know." She laughed, already calming.

His tone was warm, but tight as well. "Everything okay? You sound kinda spastic, spazzy."

She smiled at his teasing. "I guess I've got jitters, but I

wanted to hear your voice, before I saw you. You know, at the altar."

"You're sweet. I've got jitters, too. Goes with the terri-tory, right? Especially with the audience we've got watch-ing. You'll be fine."

Leigh waited a beat for something more—an "I love you," perhaps. It didn't arrive, but Dan was stressed, same as her. And like her, he didn't really know what he was doing. No script, just two young people nervous before their vows. Nor-mal. The thing Leigh ached most to be. She glanced at her ring, its diamond blinking in the morning sunlight.

"Okay," she said. "Thanks. I just needed to talk."

"Just breathe, and I'll see you before you know it. I better go. I've got my brother on the other line."

"Tell him hi. See you soon."

"Bye."

Leigh nearly hung up, but after a pause Dan added, "Babe?" He hadn't called her that in months, and the name flooded her with relief.

She held back an impulsive plea—that they run off and elope, skip all the staged drama. "Yeah?"

"Sorry about that. It was her."

Leigh's brow furrowed. "Her?"

Dan laughed. "It was Leigh. She's got bridal nerves."

She went dead numb, head enveloped by an echoing, un-natural calm as she realized he thought he was talking to someone else.

"Babe?"

This time the pet name hit her like a slap. "Yeah?" her mouth replied, disconnected from her brain.

"Don't tell me you're jealous."

"No," Leigh murmured.

"I know right where you'll be today. Every chance I get, I'll try to catch your eye. I mean, this might be us in a few years. We have to be patient. If it's supposed to happen, it'll happen. You never know."

The numbness faded, and in its place Leigh felt hot in her dress, constricted, felt tears boiling up to sting her sinuses. Her heart pounded in her ears, loud as a gong. "You never know," she whispered.

"Don't cry. I know the timing's awful, but it's not like we planned this. It's worth it, we both agreed. You and me, we'll have our time. Last night wasn't goodbye, I told you."

Leigh didn't reply.

"Okay? Allie?"

She sucked in a breath. Allie. Allie. Her mind was too blank to supply a face, a remembered mention…not that it would help. "Okay," she breathed.

"I'll miss you while I'm away. You know that."

No words came.

"I love you."

That did it. Those words Leigh needed so badly, offered to comfort some mystery woman. Some *Allie.* Her hand shook as she pushed the end button.

She stared at herself in the mirror that ran behind the marble bar, at this stranger with her face, draped in a beautiful dress. Thoughts flashed and jabbed, but the numbness reduced them to abstract concepts. There was an Allie, who'd stolen Leigh's pet name. Who'd kept Dan from taking Leigh's call for four rings, on their *wedding day.*

The shock lifted, and behind the numbness was pure pain, so sharp it seemed her heart must be coming apart, cell by cell. Strange white sequins danced before her eyes and she leaned against the bar, feeling heavy and awkward, as though suspended on strings. The dress was shrinking, an invisible corset binding her too tight to take a full breath. The room blurred, and for a moment she *knew* it was just a dream. She'd jerk awake and everything would be as it should be, spinning walls and strangling dress all vestiges of a nightmare.

The room did come back into focus. The dress relented enough for her to catch her breath, and the spots abandoned her vision. She pushed up from the bar to find the bride in the mirror peppered with red blotches, eyes wild. Leigh saw only a stranger staring back, a scared woman of twenty-seven as ignorant as she'd been at seventeen, playing dress-up in yet another glittering identity.

She clutched the phone and raised her hand, drew it back… but no. Her posture crumpled. Now wasn't the time to start smashing up hotel rooms like some out-of-control celebutante. Actually, perhaps this was the perfect time for that, but Leigh wasn't that girl, no matter what the tabloids yearned to report.

She pressed a palm over her thumping heart, scared by the sheer pain of feeling this angry, this hurt. The rage was like an animal trying to claw its way out of her chest, but she held it down, as she always did. She forced her mind to practical matters. Decisions that needed making.

She should confront Dan.

No, she couldn't.

She had to call it off. But then the press would hound her mercilessly and the whole world would find out about this.

What was the alternative? Go through with the wedding and deal with the fallout later? Her heart twisted anew, her hands trembling as she thought of faking her way through the ceremony, her jaw clenching and lips quivering as she imagined uttering her vows, hearing Dan recite his and knowing he'd already violated them. More likely, she'd run off en route to the altar in front of two videographers and an audience of hundreds, as public as humiliation got.

She rubbed at her chest, begging her heartbeat to slow. The satin seemed to mock her fingers, cool and smooth against her heated skin.

Leigh couldn't remember the last decision she'd made for herself, but all at once, and for the first time in ages, she knew what she had to do.

She had to run.

Now.

She didn't have the first clue what she wanted from her life, but she damn well knew it wasn't all this—a three-ring sham of a wedding to a man who didn't love her, a career of other people's making, a city where she couldn't enjoy a moment's anonymity.

Her suitcase waited by the door, packed with two weeks' worth of clothes and toiletries, passport and ticket in her purse, ready to go. The trip she'd so been looking forward to, the one she'd hoped would reconnect her and Dan…the mere notion was a hand around her throat. The tabloids had been salivating for Leigh's fall from grace forever, and if she was doomed to reward their persistence, she'd give them a doozy—a gen-u-ine wedding day no-show.

She switched off her phone and slipped it into her bag, with no intention of turning it back on anytime soon.

As she wheeled her case down the hall, all was quiet, the elevator empty, the lobby peaceful. No small mercy, the press not having discovered she was staying here. She hiked her dress up to her shins and marched barefoot past Reception, through the door the stony-faced porter held, and into the cool spring air. She knew which long black Town Car was hers by the driver leaning on the hood, flipping through *Variety*.

"Hector."

His brows rose and he stood, taking in her getup. "Good morning, Leigh. You're early. Very early." His familiar deep voice with its musical Haitian accent calmed her. "And you forgot your shoes. And your mother. Change of plans?"

"Change of plans" usually meant Leigh was being harangued by a reporter and needed to end an evening earlier than expected.

"Change of plans," she agreed, and climbed inside when Hector opened the door. He shut it in his firm, reassuring way and she heard a thump as he stowed her suitcase.

Once behind the wheel, he lowered the glass. He aimed the car toward the exit. "Has your mother got her own ride sorted out?"

"Don't worry about my mother. If she calls you, tell her I asked to go home, to the apartment. I need some time to think about things."

"Ah. She being a mother-of-the-bride-zilla?" Hector teased. "You need me to drive you around before we go to the estate? Dramatic entrance?" He squinted at her in the rearview mirror, possibly noticing she had no makeup on, no jewelry, that her hair was still a damp tangle and her face flushed and mottled.

"We're not going to the estate," she said, feeling strangely serene. "We're going to the airport."

"Oh?"

She nodded, steeled in her decision. "I'm going on my honeymoon. Alone."

2

WHEN THEY ARRIVED at LAX, Hector brought Leigh her suitcase and she wrestled herself out of her gown and into jeans and a T in the backseat, protected by the tinted windows. She dug her slip-ons from her luggage and glanced at her dress. It looked like the shed skin of some beautiful, mythical creature. She left it in the car.

To camouflage her identity and the tears she could feel brewing, she found and donned her big aviator shades and Giants cap. She swallowed all the rage and sadness and confusion rising in her chest, and forced a smile.

"Thanks, Hector."

"It's no trouble. Just my job."

"My mom's going to tear you a new one."

He grinned. "I know."

"Would you do one more thing for me?"

He nodded, and Leigh slid off her engagement ring and handed it to him. In place of the sadness she'd anticipated, she felt her back straightening, as though fifty pounds of pure dread had fallen from her shoulders.

"Give that to my mom or dad or to Dan, whoever you see first. And the dress. But try to avoid all of them for at least a few hours. Until I'm on a plane."

"Are you going to be okay?"

She took a deep breath. "Yeah, I'll be okay. I just need some time away. Thank goodness I'm already booked someplace where nobody'll recognize me."

He nodded and slipped her solitaire into his breast pocket. On impulse, Leigh did something she never had before—she hugged her driver. He offered a quick squeeze in return, as warm as professionalism allowed.

"You take care of yourself. I'll dodge your mother as long as I can."

She yanked up the suitcase's retractable handle. "Wish me luck that there's an earlier flight with room for me on it."

He held up two sets of crossed fingers. "Enjoy your getaway."

With a wave, Leigh said goodbye to the last familiar face she'd see for two weeks. She said goodbye to L.A., to the girl she no longer recognized as herself, and strode through the airport's sliding doors and into the unknown.

THE FLIGHT SHE CAUGHT to New York was insanely overpriced, yet well worth it to feel L.A. dropping away behind her. If any of Leigh's first-class neighbors recognized her, they were kind enough not to let on. It was the calmest six hours she'd passed in weeks, nothing but blue sky and white clouds, totally unlike the storm swirling in her head.

She'd failed to change her second flight, a smaller carrier that had no planes leaving before the one she'd already booked, the following morning. The idea of being alone in another hotel room with only her thoughts for company scared her, so she napped fitfully through the night in the airport.

She arrived in Bridgetown at lunchtime, though, sadly, her luggage did not. No clothes, no cell charger, no toiletries. Abandoned by her own belongings.

With a mighty sigh, she headed for the airport's exit. As

the doors slid open, the warm, scented air of the island enveloped her, the sun caressing her travel-weary body. By the cab stand, a group of three smiling men played steel drums. Just an extra touch to realize tourists' stereotypical expectations, but it worked. Leigh's panic faded with the song's cheerful notes.

She'd be okay. There were plenty of clothes to be purchased here in Barbados, and her sleeping cell phone had enough juice to make a handful of calls.

Speaking of calls. She dug the device from her purse and turned it on with held breath. Alerts for voice and text messages multiplied as the phone roused. Though tempted to view Dan's and find out if he'd caught on, she ignored them all, tapping out a text for her mom. I'm safe. Won't be in touch for a while. Don't worry, and please don't follow. Sorry for the stress. See you in a couple of weeks. Leigh. As soon as the message was sent, she switched off her phone for good.

Leigh had a few hours before her final flight, and she spent it wandering the shopping district, buying a knock-off designer suitcase to fill with new clothes, then ate a lunch of fried plantains from a street vendor. It was easy to stay distracted here, amid all the colors and smells and sounds. And how lovely it felt, being any old visitor to these cheerful strangers.

At two-thirty a taxi dropped her off outside the city, at an airport on the coast—a tiny terminal with a large antenna, no runway. The roadside billboard proclaimed it Bajan Fantasy Airlines. A long dock led out into the glittering water, where a seaplane—a Cessna on water skis—bobbed lazily in the waves. As far as she knew, this was the only way to get to Harrier Key. She'd picked the resort island for its seclusion, booking one of only four private villas.

She walked through the terminal's open door and into what reminded her of a bus depot. A dark-skinned woman in a salmon-pink dress stood behind a long counter, and a single passenger lounged in the waiting area, reading a newspaper. Leigh gathered her printed ticket and ID.

The woman greeted her with the gigantic Barbadian smile Leigh had gotten very used to while shopping. "Miss Bailey?"

Anonymity gone, Leigh fell back to earth with a thump. "Yes. That's me."

"I knew it! You know how I knew that?" the woman asked brightly, tapping on a keyboard.

"Not the tabloids, I hope."

She gave her a funny look. "Tabloids? Dear me, no. I know 'cause you the only woman flyin' with us this afternoon."

"Oh. Right."

More tapping. "And you're all checked in. How about Mr. Cosenza?"

She flinched. "He won't be coming."

"Oh dear."

"Yes, change of plans."

"I'm afraid the tickets are non-refundable."

"That's fine. Sorry if it's any extra trouble for you."

"Not at all. You got twenty minutes before you take off. Help yourself to coffee or tea." She nodded to a counter with carafes and a jumble of mismatched cups.

"Thanks."

Leigh filled a rainbow mug and took a seat across from the other passenger. He wore jeans, and a linen shirt with the top few buttons ignored, his tan and the state of his overgrown brown hair telling her his vacation had been going on for some time. He seemed like a man with no place to go, in no rush to get there.

He caught her staring. His eyes were as blue as the water beyond the windows, and Leigh didn't look away quickly enough to appear polite, so she smiled instead and gave a tiny wave. He smiled in response, then turned back to his paper.

Leigh tried to keep her gaze on the ocean, though she stole a glance at her fellow traveler every few seconds.

Something about his ease attracted her. Leigh had been surrounded by L.A. people for so long—a species whose males preened as diligently as its females—that this man's lack of styling struck her as refreshingly exotic. He was also nothing like Dan, which didn't hurt. Taller, she suspected, generally bigger, more fair, with those bluest of blue eyes.

For the first time in what felt like forever, Leigh let herself imagine how it might feel to kiss a man who wasn't Dan. What would he taste like? What would his skin smell like? How would his stubble feel, after she'd spent two years with a studious shaver? The fact that she could wonder such things had her breathing easier. She was hurt, not ruined.

The stranger folded his paper and called to the woman behind the desk. "Just the one, Jackie?"

"Just the one."

"Right." He turned to Leigh. "You ready to go?"

She blinked. "Go, like, take off?"

"Unless you feel like swimming."

"No, I'm ready." She drained her cup and rose to place it on the coffee counter. She looked to the man as she picked up her suitcase. "You do this a lot? Do you work on one of the islands?"

Another smile, one that gave him a dimple. "I do."

Jackie broke in. "He's your pilot, dear."

"Oooh." Leigh offered a dopey grin. "Sorry. I thought you were a passenger."

"Only if you feel like doing the flying. In which case I'll happily take a nap."

She laughed. "No, no, you do the flying."

"Okay then." He gave Jackie a salute and headed for the rear door, Leigh following him into the sunshine.

"You're American," she said.

"Guilty."

"Where are you from?"

"In some former life I recall living in New York City." If he'd ever had a jarring city accent it was gone now, and his voice matched his looks. He was easy on both the eyes and ears.

"Wow. You've made quite a lifestyle change."

He stopped short a few paces from the building and turned, crossing his arms over his chest, seeming suddenly taller. "Before I let you board, we have a little issue to clear up."

Apprehension tightened her middle. "Oh?"

"You've put me in a tricky spot."

"Did I? I'm paying for both tickets."

He shook his head, his smile more mischievous than warm, shifting all the flattering assumptions she'd too hastily made about him. "Your mother left about ten messages demanding I don't take you off this island."

Leigh frowned, feeling a touch of panic.

He leaned closer. "Bit of an awkward position for me. I'm sure you can appreciate that."

Her attention jumped everywhere, from his face to the plane to the water. "Can I bribe you?"

He straightened, expression brightening. "Sure. Knock yourself out."

She rifled through her purse, hiding her irritation. "A hundred?"

He accepted the colorful Barbadian bill and pocketed it.

Leigh released a breath, as relieved as she was annoyed. Her shopping trip had taught her that prices here were highly negotiable, a bit of island culture she might need to get savvier at, lest the locals fleece her at every opportunity. This latest swindle set her back about fifty American dollars, but no price was too high, not in exchange for getting her where she needed to be.

"So we can go?"

"We can." He led her down the long aluminum dock. The plane was small, its bottom half painted a cheerful aqua, top half gleaming white and emblazoned with the name *The Passport*.

Leigh's unscrupulous pilot looked over his shoulder. "The rumor mill at the resort said this is your honeymoon."

"It is."

"Think you may have forgotten to pack your husband. Or did he get misplaced in transit?"

She smiled to cover the pang she felt. "Change of plans."

WHEN THEY REACHED the plane, Will took Leigh's bag and stowed it in the cabin. She traveled light, for a celebrity. He pictured her faceless fiancé back in L.A., sitting on a bed beside a pile of clothes and swimsuits that also hadn't made the cut. Poor bastard.

Will hopped back down to the dock. "Just you and me, so you have a choice—sit back here or play copilot."

"Which is better?"

"Tough to beat the view in the cockpit."

Tough to beat a chance to have her as his captive audience, as well. He might not get many chances like this again, and he was secretly pleased when she said, "Okay. Sure."

He secured the cabin and she followed him to the front, fumbling her way up the short ladder that connected the float to the cockpit. She settled into the far seat, taking in the console and instruments. When Will buckled himself in and donned sunglasses, she followed suit. She squinted at his license, displayed in a plastic frame mounted above the windshield.

"William Burgess."

"*Captain* William Burgess," he corrected officiously. "But Will is fine."

"Leigh Bailey."

He offered his finest pilot's handshake, decisive and confident, qualities a person ought to value in a man charged with transporting her across sea and sky.

As Will prepped for takeoff, Leigh reached out to touch the panel of a gauge on the console. Scowling, he snatched her hand away and set it firmly on her knee.

"Don't get handsy," he said, pulling a cloth from a compartment and buffing away whatever fingerprints Leigh may have left on the glass. He might not dress like a captain, but this plane was more than his meal ticket—it was his baby. And he didn't let strangers poke and prod and leave smudges on his baby.

Leigh frowned, looking annoyed. "Sorry."

After a brief safety spiel, Will started *The Passport,* and soon enough the beaches of Barbados were slipping by from several hundred feet up. He wondered what she was thinking, given her intent gaze. Maybe the same things he always did—all that sand, all that water. All this, all to herself.

He spoke over the drone of the engine. "You didn't need to bribe me, you know."

She frowned again.

"It's *your* name on the ticket. Doesn't bother me if your old lady's got her panties in a twist about what you're up to." He flashed her a grin, one that made her cheeks flush from discomfort, he guessed. "Want your money back?"

"Nah. You earned it." Her casual tone was a put-on, Will could tell.

"Must be nice to be able to take or leave a hundred bucks."

"I suppose."

"Nice to be able to take or leave a husband." It was a mean jab, he knew, but bound to earn him a response, a bit of information about his passenger. Maybe a sound slap, had he not been operating a plane. "So which did you do?" Will prompted. "Take him or leave him?"

"I left him," she said coolly.

"Good for you. Hope you've got a lovely settlement coming to you." An even lower blow, but Will had accepted a generous offer to collect information on this woman, and he didn't like the thought of tweezing it out with some sympathetic, smooth-talker act. He'd goad it out of her. At least that way he wouldn't be exploiting some false confidence.

Her face burned and she turned to glare at him. "That's a really rude thing to say."

"Is it?"

"Yes, it's *really* rude."

"Good thing I don't fly for tips."

She blinked, clearly incredulous, and shook her head. All that friendliness she'd showed him in the terminal fell away, surely sinking deep beneath the waves below.

"Not too late to swim, if you're offended by the service."

"No, thank you. Though I suspect I'll be sitting in the cabin on the way back."

"Probably wise. My old man was a cabbie in New York. My gifts of customer service are purely genetic."

"A very rare and malicious disorder, I'm sure. Thank goodness you're not contagious."

He grinned, rather enjoying the dig.

"And since you're so nosy, you may as well know there's no settlement, because I didn't get married."

Will swallowed. "Duly noted." He'd expected to feel some kind of triumph at such an informational coup, but he didn't. It actually felt bad, a nauseous little twist in his gut.

"I was just teasing, you know." Will met her eyes as much as was possible through two pairs of shades. "Taking the edge off?"

"More like sharpening it."

"Not my intention."

"I hope your landing approaches are smoother than your social ones."

"Sorry." He didn't make an effort to sound especially sorry. Nausea notwithstanding, the tactless approach was working. "I've never had a runaway Hollywood bride in that seat before."

She pursed her lips. "Do you know who I am?"

Enough to know some sleazebag back in L.A. will pay good money to hear what you're up to. "There's only a few types who vacation at this place, and when they're women coming from Los Angeles, I can usually narrow it to actress or model or Hollywood wife. And we've ruled out wife."

Leigh held her tongue.

"Not that I need to know," Will said with a theatrical sigh of disinterest. "I'm just the chauffeur."

Leigh countered with a haughtiness that struck him as unpracticed. "I have a chauffeur, sometimes, and he's far better at diplomacy than you."

"I have no doubt." Will gave her another searching look. She wasn't the woman he'd been expecting, and fruitful though it was, she didn't deserve the antagonism...but he couldn't deny he liked the way his teasing made her cheeks go pink. Still, he softened his tone. "Don't take this personally if you can help it, but I didn't have you pegged as a woman scorned."

"No?"

He shook his head. "More like an escapee. Thought maybe I was your getaway driver."

Her lips parted, but no reply followed. Her look said he was right, that she had escaped. From what, Will couldn't guess, but one thing seemed clear—her flight was no publicity stunt.

He felt another pang in his middle.

Will had designed his life as free from obligations and guilt as humanly possible, expressly to avoid the ugly emotions he felt now. He didn't want to report on this woman anymore, but at the end of the day, she was nothing to him. He needed the money for things that mattered. Things that mattered far more than a few innocuous tidbits leaked to some slimeball editor thousands of miles away in Hollywood.

Leigh's hackles seemed to lower. "You are," she finally said. "You're my getaway driver."

She relaxed back into her seat and they were quiet for ten minutes or more.

Will pointed into the distance. "See that?"

Leigh squinted at a dot in the turquoise ocean. "Is that it?"

"Yup. That's your hideout."

"Wow. That *is* private."

"Eleven square miles of paradise. Nothing but white sand and swaying palms and room service."

"Sounds heavenly. Though it's probably nothing exotic to you."

Will laughed. "Are you kidding? I've lived on that tiny speck for seven years now, and I still wake up every day pinching myself." The second he abandoned the prying, the sourness in his stomach eased.

"You live there?"

He nodded. "Fly people back and forth twice a day for a passable stipend."

"Wow."

"You say that a lot, you know."

"Oh. Yes, I suppose I do."

"You're very easy to impress," Will said as the plane began its descent. "I like that in a woman."

"Yes. That would be a requisite for a man of your charms."

He laughed again, then realized he might be in danger of actually liking Leigh Bailey, celebrity runaway bride or not. That didn't bode well for his gig.

The island grew closer, and Will could make out two of the villas from this angle, two tiny blue swimming pools, two docks poking out into the waves.

"So you *are* famous, right?" he asked, banking the plane left.

"Not crazy-famous. B-list, I guess. Maybe B plus."

"What are you famous for?" She'd been in some films he'd never heard of, but that was all he knew about her.

"When I was in high school, outside San Francisco, I was really into dance. And one summer I was fed up over not getting called back for theater auditions, so my mom drove me to L.A. to try out for a movie. And I got it."

"What kind of movie?"

"About a shy, bookworm girl who goes away for a summer to Miami and meets all these hot-blooded ballroom dancers, and falls in love with this boy. Just another star-crossed teen romance with a dance-off at the end. That's what I'm most known for. And I did a few romantic comedies and a couple indie films, and got talked into a cosmetics campaign. But nothing hugely amazing."

"Looking to be the next big thing?"

"Quite the opposite."

Will's brow furrowed in surprise, and he hoped she didn't notice.

"I'd happily wake up tomorrow as a complete nobody."

"I hate to break it to you, but running away from your wedding's not gonna do much to keep you out of the spotlight."

"No kidding."

"But if you're looking to be a nobody, you've picked the best place on earth to do it."

"Actually… You let me bribe you into taking me this far. Any chance I can bribe you into keeping your mouth shut to any other passengers or resort staff?"

"Discretion comes standard. In fact, I've already forgotten your name, Miss…?"

She smiled grimly, and Will tried to ignore the fresh stab of guilt his lie triggered.

AFTER A SHAKY LANDING, Will climbed out and secured the craft to a long aluminum dock, then offered Leigh a hand as she disembarked.

"Thanks."

He fetched her suitcase and made a beeline for a huge stucco building with terra-cotta roof tiles and a grand arched entryway. She followed, breathing in the sea-scented island air as the plane's diesel smell faded. She took in the white sand, blue sky, her pilot's backside…the latter merely to spite Dan. Not because she still had *any* lingering curiosity about kissing this galling man. Certainly not. Though Will did retain some appeal. She'd gotten so used to everyone telling her what they thought she wanted to hear, Will's tactlessness had a strange allure.

He held the door as they reached the reception building, the lobby equal parts posh and primitive with its huge windows and fountain and exotic plants.

He set her suitcase before the unmanned reception counter and tapped a silver bell.

"Thank you," Leigh said.

Will didn't leave, and she bit her lip. His proximity made her feel funny. Naked. "Sorry. *Am* I supposed to tip you?"

He smiled. "I'm driving you to your villa, once you've checked in."

"You do that, too?"

"I do for that unit. It's not far from my place."

"Okay."

"And you may tip me for that, incidentally."

Leigh's retort was cut off as a harried young Caribbean woman appeared.

"So sorry to keep you waitin'. Mrs. Cosenza?" Ah, another dagger in the breast.

"Miss Bailey," Will corrected, tucking his hands in his pockets.

The woman looked to Leigh. "Oh?"

"Yes, just me. It's under Cosenza, but I... Well, anyhow. Change of plans." She ought to have that printed on a T-shirt.

The woman got busy typing. "So only one key, then. No problem at all. You're in the Shearwater Villa." She procured a plastic card and swiped it across a device before handing it to Leigh. "Let me jus' get a driver 'round for you."

"I'm on it," Will said.

The woman frowned first at him, then Leigh. "You really want this bum escortin' you?"

Leigh looked from one to the other.

The woman laughed. "Just kiddin'—you're in good hands. Terrible vehicle, but very good hands. Now anything you need, you'll find the phone numbers in the binder waitin' on your coffee table. You have a lovely visit, miss."

Leigh followed Will outside to a small parking lot.

He held up her suitcase. "Anything delicate in here?"

"Nope."

"Good."

They walked past several shiny white SUVs to a rusty old pickup. Will put her bag in the bed. He opened the passenger side and once again Leigh buckled herself in as copilot.

Will slid behind the wheel. Just to test him, she tapped the dashboard provocatively.

"Go nuts. It's only the plane I'm a fascist about." The truck started with a mournful noise. He drove them onto a smooth gravel road, heading inland. Leigh unrolled her window to hear the birds and welcome the sun on her arm.

"Final leg of your great escape," Will said.

She nodded.

"How long do you get to play fugitive, before you turn yourself in?"

"Two weeks."

"Very nice."

Already this place had her pain fading to a dull throb. Reality could shove it, as long as she was in paradise. She smiled at the decadence of the idea and shut her eyes, angling her face to catch the sunshine.

"Two weeks of surf and sand and rum," Will said, giving voice to her thoughts.

"And silence."

"My mistake."

"We have plenty of surf and sand and rum in Los Angeles, anyway. I picked this place for the seclusion." She turned to smirk at him. "How did you end up down here, anyhow?"

He made a face as though he'd never considered it before. "Got my pilot's license when I was nineteen, moved to Cancún. Moved to Nassau. San Juan. Woke up here seven years ago."

Sounded a bit like Leigh's life, waking up somewhere unexpected…only this man had flown himself to his destination, whereas she'd merely let herself be shuttled. She was done being swept. She might not know where she ultimately wanted to end up, but she'd brought herself this far, and against everyone's wishes. Felt awfully good. She eyed Will's hands on the wheel, wishing she was driving.

The truck trundled out of a small palm forest and past a tiny settlement of colorful houses on stilts, all of the milling residents unmistakably island people. Will raised his hand at everyone who greeted him, and engaged in a playful fake argument with one of the men, laughing as he turned his attention back to the road. How weird it must be to live someplace where friends were the vast majority of the people one encountered, strangers the oddities. Weird and comforting.

"What is that…area?"

"The shanty town? That's where all us commoners hang out when we're not fluffing your pillows or spit-shining your bidets."

"A whole town, just to make the visitors at four measly villas happy…"

"Easier said than done."

She got stuck staring at his arm for a moment, tanned skin and trim muscle beside cream-colored linen. "Which came first, the town or the resort?"

"Resort. This place was human-free until it got developed fifteen years ago."

"What's there to do in town?"

Will laughed. "For you? Nothing. Just a bunch of rowdy resort rats drinking and dancing and saying all the stuff we're not allowed to when guests are within earshot."

"Dancing?"

"Stick with the spa treatments. Your villa's got everything you'll need, a speed-dial for your every whim."

"Maybe my whims don't come on silver platters," Leigh said, and the skeptical, bawdy glance Will shot her made heat bloom unbidden in her middle. She took her shades off to glare at him properly. "Not like that, Captain Pervert. Just, I don't know. Maybe I'd like to get out and explore. Meet the locals."

"If you wanted that, you wouldn't have come to this place. But if you need a lift to Bridgetown I leave here at ten and two, seven days a week. Plus special trips for a steep fee. Can't fly after dark, so book a place to stay on the mainland if you're looking to party."

She nodded, committing the times to memory.

"Here we are," Will announced, driving them up to a

stately yet modern stucco building with vast windows—so vast Leigh could see the ocean clear through the other side. "Wow."

"*Wow...*" Will echoed, pulling around the circular drive. They exited and he carried her suitcase up a set of wide stone steps.

"Thank you." Leigh checked that her key card worked, setting her bag inside before rooting through her purse.

Will shook his head. "Don't."

"No tip?"

"Your earlier gratuity was more than generous."

"Oh. Well, thanks for the lift."

"Enjoy your stay. See you when you're ready to head back to the mainland."

She put out her hand and he accepted it. That sure shake, his skin as warm as his dangerous smile. A curious, *vengeful* part of Leigh imagined that confident touch elsewhere on her body. A new man's unfamiliar palms on her bare skin, for the first time in two years... Realizing their shake had gone on too long, she released his hand.

"See you around," she said lamely.

"I suspect you will. Enjoy your escape."

"I'll try."

He offered a polite smile, then trotted down the steps, not looking back as he climbed into his truck and drove away.

The second he disappeared past a stand of palms, Leigh missed him. Not Will, the person, but the sort of person he was—one who didn't give half a damn who *she* was.

She carried her bag through the entryway and into a sunken living room that opened to a solarium at one end, overlooked by the mosaic-paneled counter of a gleaming kitchen on the other. The villa was only one story, but the cathedral ceiling and tall windows made it feel doubly spacious. Plush furniture, massive television mounted on one wall, cut lilies filling the air with the heady smell of the tropics.

She wandered through the living room and found the master bedroom. Its far wall was nothing but glass, looking out onto her patio with its pool and hot tub, pristine white beach and aquamarine ocean beyond.

The place was jaw-droppingly gorgeous. Island-exotic but L.A.-stylish, peaceful, ordered, quiet…

Too quiet.

It was far too easy to get lost in one's thoughts here, and Leigh was eager to get lost *outside* her head, at least until the stinging open wound of recent events scabbed over.

She made herself busy, unpacking straight away. To her surprise, she found a crumpled hundred dollar bill in her suitcase. She smoothed it, conjuring Will's smirk. "Freak."

She called Reception and gave instructions for how to field any calls. *Miss Bailey is enjoying her vacation, and does not wish to be disturbed. If you leave a message, we will be sure it reaches her.* Just the right mix of stern and casual, so hopefully, she'd be left alone, but not cause *too* huge a panic.

That first evening passed in beautifully appointed boredom. Leigh napped, waded in the surf, ordered a delicious dinner and admirably resisted both the TV and her phone. She was going through the motions of relaxation, but didn't feel any of their effects.

This was surely the longest in years she'd gone without seeing a familiar face, and she hadn't counted on how lonely she'd feel, how small and insecure. The solitude was supposed to clear her head, but her worries seemed to echo all the more loudly. Now and then she nearly missed Dan…but no. She merely missed her old life, that comfortable lie she'd grown so accustomed to living.

LEIGH SLEPT POORLY, reading on the couch until she fell into fitful dreams full of dress fittings and ocean waves.

The next morning, her doorbell chimed as she was brushing her teeth. She crossed the lounge, spotting Will Burgess's truck through the window. Her stomach gave a funny flutter. She was clearly hard up for company, to feel a rush at the prospect of a conversation with the most abrasive man she'd met in ages. Sexy, sure, but undeniably tactless.

Toothbrush in hand, she opened the door.

Will's eyes were hidden by sunglasses, and stacked atop his pair were another—Leigh's. "Good morning, valued guest."

"Good morning, sketchy pilot."

He took off both sets of glasses and handed hers over. "You left those in my truck yesterday."

"Thanks. You left your bribe in my bag."

He grinned, and Leigh was tempted to don her shades to protect herself from his extraordinary eyes.

"Must have fallen out of my pocket."

"And into my zipped suitcase."

"The mysteries of physics. You've got a little…" Will gestured at the corner of his mouth.

Leigh wiped at her lips, at whatever toothpaste he saw.

"Other side."

She tried again.

"That got it." Will leaned against the door frame. "Must be hard not having your butler around to let you know when you've got stuff on your face."

She rolled her eyes.

"How did you cope, brushing your own teeth?"

"Are you waiting for a tip, Captain? Because the more you talk, the crappier your chances are getting."

"Just being friendly. Customer service and all that. Anything you need?"

Company was the only thing Leigh really craved, but she

wouldn't admit it to this man. "Only if you know how the coffeemaker works. It's so high-tech I couldn't figure it out."

"I can operate a plane, so let's hope it's not beyond me."

Leigh stepped aside and he strolled to the device.

"Damn, that is high-tech."

She watched as he messed around with the digital features. His laid-back charisma seemed even more obvious amid the kitchen's sleekness. What Leigh had felt in the terminal the previous afternoon hadn't been a fluke, or a simple matter of revenge—she was attracted to him. But it was a purely physical attraction, signifying nothing more than the fact that he was *slightly* sexier than he was annoying.

After much poking, he got the machine hissing and gurgling and coffee began to fill the pot.

Will gestured between the machine and himself, making a great show of his accomplishment. "How about that? All it needed was a retinal scan and two forms of ID."

"Thanks."

"Just make sure you select a mode. I think that's the only trick. Anything else you need?"

"No, I'm good. Thanks for bringing my sunglasses."

"Anytime."

She was on the verge of inviting him to stay for a coffee, but he spoke first, sparing her from sounding pathetic.

"I better head in for the morning flight."

"Yes, you better."

She walked him to the door, trying to ignore the shape of his shoulders beneath his shirt, the disarming, masculine rhythm of his easy gait.

"Thanks again."

He gave her a salute and headed down the steps to his truck. "Enjoy your coffee," he called, slamming his door.

"Enjoy your flight."

He draped his tan arm along the open window as the engine groaned to life.

Leigh closed her door and listened until the truck was gone, then sank up to her neck in lonely silence. She poured a coffee and flipped through the resort's activities guide, nothing sparking her interest. Nowhere in the many descriptions did it say, "Interact with other humans before you lose your mind! Don't forget to bring a towel."

She shut the binder, more listless than ever. All she wanted was what Will had just offered—company. No pampering or butt-kissing, no star treatment. She wished he'd come back, but there was no good reason for him to. She'd just have to settle for a masseuse or horseback riding instructor.... But she was sick to death of things being done for her, services offered by supremely nice people who probably just gossiped about her once she'd gone.

Then something occurred to Leigh. She didn't have to wait for Will to come back to enjoy a taste of the candid, easy company she craved. She could go after what she wanted herself. After all, what had playing by the rules done for her lately?

3

As THE SUN DIPPED LOWER, Leigh's mood rose higher and higher.

A shower washed away the salt from her afternoon swim, and her hastily acquired shorts and funky halter top enveloped her in a sense of blessed unfamiliarity. The smell of sunscreen had her craving a cold drink, perhaps one with an umbrella in it, served in half a pineapple or some other delightful cliché.

When the clock chimed five-thirty she grabbed her new sandals, carrying them as she walked down the beach. Just as she'd hoped, after a twenty minutes' stroll she spotted the workers' settlement farther along the shore.

Will's clunky old truck was parked just off the road, and Leigh followed a wooden walkway through the grass and sand to a dwelling yards from the high tide's edge. Tinny music played from an unseen radio, and she spotted its owner as she neared.

He was straddling an upside-down canoe raised on blocks beside the building, sanding away a coat of peeling paint. It seemed there was no limit to how casual his wardrobe could get. He was dressed in khaki cutoffs, a plaid button-up shirt left completely open to flap about his arms in the warm breeze. He swept his shaggy hair from his eyes and Leigh had to admire the greater whole of him. Tan and lean, that mischievously handsome face looking placid for a change, his attention focused on his project. His well-past-five-o'clock shadow and bare feet made her envy his life with a fresh pang.

She clapped the soles of her sandals together. "Knock knock."

Will glanced up from his task with a grin. "Well, look who's here. You get lost on the way to a hot-rock massage?"

"Is this where you live, Captain?" She nodded to the cottage on stilts. "It's adorable."

Will glowered, faking insult.

"Sorry. It's butch. Really butch."

He set aside the sanding block and wiped his palms on his shorts. "What can I do for you, Miss Bailey? Need a lift to civilization?"

"No."

"Thank goodness for that." He reached to the windowsill and took a deep swig from a bottle of beer. "How was that coffee?"

"Just fine, thank you."

"You walk all the way here?"

"It's only about a half mile."

"Didn't know your kind walked."

She shot him a snobby look, meandering closer. "My kind?"

His smile sharpened to a smirk, one that stirred Leigh's pulse. "Yeah, your kind, little miss movie star."

"Well, you were misinformed. My kind does plenty more than walk. I came to ask you about the dancing you mentioned yesterday."

His brows rose. "That's what you came here for? Dancing?"

"Sure. It's my favorite thing in the world. Or it used to be."

"And here I thought maybe you'd missed me."

"Again, you're greatly misinformed."

"I don't know what you're thinking of, but the dancing here isn't what you're after. More like stand-up dry-humping."

Leigh pictured such a thing. "Sounds like a movie I starred in."

Another of those deadly, snarky smiles. "What happened in the movie?"

"The annoying pilot told the charming actress where to find a cold drink and a good beat."

"Of course he did." Damn, that dimple.

She kicked at the sand. "So, will you tell me?"

"I'll do better than that. I'll take you."

"Yeah?"

"Sure, what the hell."

She smiled. "Thank you. It's way too quiet back in my villa."

"I'll get chewed out if any managers think I invited you to fraternize with us lowly workers."

"Then tell them the truth—that I forced myself on you."

His lips twitched, as though he was holding back a remark, a flirtation. Just that tiny hesitation from this shameless man brought a warmth to Leigh's skin, one that had nothing to do with the late afternoon sun.

"I'll bribe you," she offered.

"No more bribes. Plus I'll get chewed out worse by management if they hear I failed to chaperone you, out among us uncivilized natives." Will slid down from the canoe.

"Is this what you do with your free time? Fix up old boats?" Leigh ran a hand over the point where rough paint met smooth wood, and stole a glance at Will's bare chest while he stowed tools.

"I do all sorts of stuff. And I work less than four hours a day, so I do a *lot* of all sorts of stuff."

"No TV?"

"I don't have one. Very little worth watching."

"That's for sure." Leigh imagined what would have happened if she'd stayed in her villa—check room service for peanut butter availability, then scour the channels for news about herself. Pathetic, toxic habit. Tomorrow she'd phone and see if the satellite could be disconnected for the duration of her stay.

She waited while Will disappeared inside his house. The radio went silent and he emerged carrying a cooler, with a pair of sandals on top of it.

"What's in there?"

"Essentials." He headed up the walkway, dropping his sandals to the ground as they reached the rough gravel road and slipping them on. Leigh did the same.

"Thanks," she said.

Will shrugged, setting ice inside the cooler rattling. "I would have ended up there eventually anyhow, with or without you."

"Where are we going?"

"To Bethany and Oscar's place."

"And they work here, too?"

"That's a given. Bethany's a chef, Oscar manages the drivers."

"They throw lots of parties?"

"It's not that organized around here. People finish work, take a nap or smoke a joint—"

"Or sand a boat."

"Or that. Then you wander toward wherever the ruckus is coming from. But I know it'll be there tonight, since it's Monday. Always something happening at their place on a Monday."

A girl ran past them, followed by a smaller one, both shrieking with laughter.

"That little one was theirs," Will said.

"Cute." Leigh craned her neck to watch the kids disappear between the trees. "How often do us guests turn up at your get-togethers?"

"Rarely. Especially ones like you," Will said with a tight, self-satisfied smile.

"Ones like me? Go on, tell me what that means, since I know you're dying to."

"Just that you're a girl. Most of the guests who party-crash are older men, looking to escape their wives' idea of a vacation. But they're rare, as well. You're just extra rare. Like how I like my steak."

She laughed. "How old are you, anyway?"

"Thirty-three."

She nodded, not sure what she'd been expecting. He lived a life she'd normally have ascribed to either a younger man, not yet compelled to shape up and find a "real" job, or an older one sick of the rat race. "What's it like, living in a postcard?"

Will stared over the water for a moment, and Leigh studied his eyes in the dying sun, bright as a blue glass pendant she'd admired in the shopping district the previous morning. She wondered who had raised this man and given him those eyes, and what they thought of the life he'd made for himself, so far from New York City.

"It's lovely," he finally said.

"What's the least lovely thing about it?"

"Hurricanes."

"I mean, like, from day to day."

"Honestly, there's not much. Bit of a pain getting hold of certain things. Costs an arm and a leg to have stuff shipped from the States. Hence all the bribes you'll see going down around here."

"What sorts of things? What do you miss?"

"Aren't you just brimming with questions?"

She smiled at him. "I'm desperate for human contact."

"You must be, if you came to me. So much for your dreams of seclusion."

"So what do you miss?"

He pondered it. "I miss watching the Knicks play. Can't buy that off a guy in Bridgetown."

"Well, I'm sure I get that channel at my place. Feel free to come watch a game, in exchange for tonight's party."

He met her gaze squarely for a breath. "I may just take you up on that."

"You'll have to make it worth my while, of course." She rubbed her fingers together and bobbed her eyebrows at him, as silly as she'd been with anyone in weeks.

"You'll fit in just fine here, Miss Bailey."

Their gazes lingered longer than was casual before they turned back to the road. Leigh felt that heat again, the one she wished was as simple as sunburn. This time it had nothing to do with revenge, a shift that felt at once joyous and dangerous.

"That's it." Will nodded to the farthest house in the settlement, bigger than his own but also on stilts, with rounded lavender shingles like fish scales. Tiki torches were lit along the beach, a grill smoking and a dozen people milling around it, cups and beer bottles waving as arms gestured. The breeze carried their laughter, and the aromas of sizzling meat and ocean breeze and that distinctive Caribbean scent, of flowers and sand and the vastness of the sky here. Leigh breathed it in, drank in the color of the clouds as dusk approached. She filled herself with this place, so full there'd be no room for a single bad thought.

Will kicked off his sandals at the roadside as they headed for the beach. He glanced at her. "Ready?"

She looked at the people. "Sure. Seems calm enough to me."

He grinned. "Wait till the sun goes down."

"You guys can't be crazier than the nutjobs back in L.A."

They rounded the house to the beach, and a few partygoers cheered as they spotted Will.

"Everyone!" he bellowed. "There is royalty among us peas-
ants this evening."

More cheers and a few whistles sounded, and a couple of
bottles raised in Leigh's direction.

"Her highness wants a taste of how the real islanders live,"
Will went on with an indulgent grin. "So do be on your worst
behavior."

He led Leigh across the warm sand and set his cooler near
the grill. A tall, big-bellied man greeted him with a hand
clasp and a slap on the back before turning his smile on the
party's newcomer.

"Oscar, this is Leigh, staying at Shearwater. Leigh, this is
Oscar, your host for this evening."

She shook Oscar's hand. "Nice to meet you."

"And you." His attention shifted as Will pulled two shining blue fish from the cooler. "Ah, beauties! Bethany will
be pleased."

Will handed off the gift and rinsed his hands in the ice.
Oscar left them to deliver the fish to the immensely pregnant
woman manning the grill.

"You caught those?" Leigh asked Will.

He nodded. "I go out most mornings. Motorboat, not
canoe."

"Wow." She caught it this time, mocking herself before
Will got the chance. *"Wow...."*

He smiled. "Get you a drink? Cocktail? Beer?"

Not sure she was ready for whatever filled people's plastic tumblers, she opted for a beer. Following Will inside to a
bustling kitchen, she smiled nervously at the other guests as
he found her a bottle. She was introduced in warmly teasing
tones, a flurry of names and faces. Leigh's nerves returned,

seeing how intimately they all knew one another, how laughter seemed to quiet when her guest status was announced.

She leaned close to Will. "Is it making people uncomfortable, my being here?"

"Uncomfortable is too strong. Not like the boss is in the room. But you do change the atmosphere. You've got the power to complain."

"I don't want to spoil anyone's good time." And she certainly didn't want to be anyplace where'd she feel once again like an outsider.

Will nudged her with his elbow. "Give them a few more drinks, an hour or so to get used to you. Just be yourself."

"Be myself." Whoever that was. Leigh straightened, sipping her beer and deciding to do just what he'd said. She *did* know who she was. It was her family and Dan and all those strangers in Hollywood who'd tricked her into believing she was someone else, someone different, some face off a screen or magazine spread.

Outside, a drum sounded. Will nodded to the exit and she preceded him into the cooler air, the darkening evening. She met a few more people, all polite but unmistakably distant once they learned she was a paying guest. She and Will wandered to the water's edge, until they were wading in the sea, sipping their drinks, watching the torchlight bouncing off the dark waves that lapped at their shins. They'd both gone quiet, and Leigh wondered how much of a damper she was putting on *his* evening.

Will cleared his throat before asking, "So, do you regret it? Leaving him?"

She met his gaze, shocked. Shocked he'd been wondering something so personal, so sentimental, and equally surprised to realize the question hadn't yet crossed her mind. But the answer needed no speculation. It would be ages before she could feel anything good about Dan. Though she hoped she could eventually forgive him, she knew he was now a figment purely of the past. "No, I don't regret it."

Will nodded, expression neutral as he turned his attention back to shore.

Leigh exhaled a long and melancholy sigh, and in its wake she felt relief unknotting her muscles. "It would've been a huge mistake if I'd gone through with it. The way I realized I couldn't marry him… It hurts, anyhow. It's humiliating and complicated, but once all that fades, I'll be happy with my decision."

"You seem like you've got a good head on your shoulders."

"For a celebrity," Leigh said wryly.

"For anybody." He sipped his drink, not meeting her eyes. "How could you end up at the altar with any doubt in your mind?"

"It's hard to explain. You have to think of fame as a drug. It does stuff to your head. It gets you sort of drunk or high, and reality's modified. Especially when everyone around you seems to see things the same way." She watched the quavering reflection of her calves in the water. "Like you're all seeing the world in a funhouse mirror, but everyone agrees that it looks the same, so you just… You get used to the warp, I guess."

"Enough to marry the wrong man?"

"Nearly. I know, it sounds awful."

"Sounds typical, though. The Hollywood crowd aren't known for their stellar marital track record."

Leigh nodded. "My fiancé—the guy he used to be, anyhow—I would've married him, no hesitation. But by the time the big day arrived, he was different. And it's so easy in that world to tell yourself, 'things will be normal again, after X happens.' Your movie wraps or the ink dries on your next contract. But X happens and things *don't* just go back to normal.

Normal is something you opt out of when you sign up to be part of the entertainment business."

"Lots of people dream of having what you do."

"I know they do."

"But not you."

She sipped her beer, considering. "I never wanted to be famous. I was seventeen and all I wanted to do was dance, and maybe see if I could build a life out of it. The fame was a fluke, but it had its own momentum, especially when I saw how proud it made my parents. I'm sort of a people pleaser. Okay, I'm a *massive* people pleaser."

Will laughed, the rich sound as relaxing as the alcohol. As warm and intimate as she imagined his breath might feel on her neck.

"It's hard for me to admit I don't want any of it anymore," Leigh said, "knowing how ungrateful so many people would say I was if I quit."

"Fans, you mean?"

"Fans, sure. But there's way more guilt about your family, for whatever they may have sacrificed. And from all the people who believed in your talent, pushed you and promoted you. But I also know I'm expendable. I'm not the 'it' girl-next-door, twenty-year-old actress anymore."

He finally met her eyes, his blue ones seeming as bright in the torchlight as they were in the sunshine. "Washed up at twenty-five? That's harsh."

"Twenty-seven, but yeah. I'm a certain kind of commodity, and my time's peaked. There's an army of perky replacements happy to take my old roles."

"Ouch."

She laughed. "Yeah, my expiration date's fast approaching."

They shared a smile, again lingering just longer than was innocent. Her gaze moved to his bare chest before she got hold of herself and turned to watch the party on the beach. People were eating and laughing, and more musicians had joined the drummer, as children danced in the sand.

"So what do you want to do?" Will asked. "If your dream of becoming a nobody comes true."

She kept her eyes on the party. "I want to dance."

"Like on stage or—"

"No, right now. I want to dance." No thoughts of what to do once she got home. Just enjoy the present, the simple pleasures of this place.

She sloshed to shore and left her bottle in a milk crate full of empties. The two children who'd run past earlier were hopping and gyrating before the band, and as Leigh approached they looked up at her, curious.

"What's the best dance you guys know?" Leigh asked them.

After a pause, the older child demonstrated her moves, a hip-thrusting motion accompanied by a rolling of her narrow shoulders, bawdy if not for the fact the kid was only about ten. Leigh mimicked the choreography, earning herself a hesitant grin.

"Look, look," said the younger girl. She offered her own signature moves, something equally raunchy she must have stolen from a music video. Leigh gave it a go, until the little girl dissolved into giggles.

"What?"

The child pointed to Leigh's butt.

"You got no ass," said the older girl.

Leigh laughed, faking offense. "Sure I do."

"You all flat back there. Like all them skinny, rich white ladies."

"I can't help that."

"You oughta eat more," the smaller girl announced loudly,

earning a reprimand and waggle of grill tongs from her mother. "Sorry."

"Anyhow," Leigh said, "you can dance with whatever size butt you've got. Show me any moves you have, I bet I can do them as well as you."

"Bet you can't," the older girl taunted.

"Bet I can. Go on, let's see what you've got."

Will wandered over. "Careful, girls. She was in a movie about a dancer and everything."

For a stinging second, his comment made Leigh feel like even more of an outsider, but she was grateful for the credibility it seemed to earn her with this tough crowd. Two sets of eyes widened. "You was in a movie?"

"I was. And I was the star. It was about a girl who learned how to tango. You want to see?"

Vigorous nods answered her.

Leigh demonstrated a flourish of moves, and her skeptical audience warmed before her eyes.

"That's cool," the bossy girl said. "How you do that?"

Leigh offered lessons, accepted tips in return from her young acquaintances. Before long the grown-ups were finishing their dinners and fetching fresh drinks, dancing in pairs on the sand. Seeking a partner of her own, Leigh scanned the growing crowd, but found Will busy at the grill, giving their pregnant hostess a break. No matter.

Leigh danced by herself, enjoying the beat and the atmosphere, the flicker of firelight and the deep indigo of the sky overhead. She shut her eyes, absorbing the laughter and music, feeling free in a way she hadn't in years. Feeling a high no vice Hollywood traded in could ever touch. Just some nobody girl, dancing on some nowhere beach. Just Leigh, for the first time in forever.

Across the sand, Will caught her eye again, laughing at a friend's joke. That damnable smile… Her energy shifted, dropping low in her belly, warm and curious, and Leigh wondered if maybe it wasn't high time to get busy making some bad decisions.

4

WILL DITCHED HIS PLATE in the kitchen. Leigh ought to get herself some dinner before they ran out…or maybe she was planning on a late-night call to room service, not this lowbrow fare. Still, at the moment she was doing a fine impression of lowbrow herself. She was dancing with Rex, one of the younger drivers, and watching gave Will a funny pang.

Jealousy was too strong a diagnosis, as was *concern*. Let the girl have her fun. He only hoped she didn't go too nuts, as celebrities seemed so fond of doing.

He wandered closer, if only to keep an eye on her. Well, fine—to have a better *view* of her. This not-quite guest, his not-quite date, the answer to his financial prayers…though he had yet to do a thing with what she'd told him in the plane. Just now it was hard to remember who she was supposed to be to him. Skin pale as the sand, smile bright as the torches. The hesitant, haunted girl he'd met on the mainland was gone, along with her street clothes, a vibrant creature now inhabiting her body. Will couldn't for the life of him put his finger on who this woman really was, and until he did, he couldn't bring himself to sell any details to the press, not even harmless ones.

But whoever she was, it was exciting to watch her body

moving this way, at once rhythmic and chaotic, like the waves. Will knew better than anybody how intoxicating this place was. He'd been high for seven years now.

What would those stupid tabloids make of her? *Runaway Bride Dances the Night Away with Resort Staff.* Some picture of her, long hair whipping wildly. Some shot that made her look drunk despite the fact she'd yet to open a second beer. No photo would convey what he saw—a woman lost in her own infectious joy. The way a bride ought to look, dancing at her wedding.

Will remembered how he'd felt the first time he'd set foot on a beach like this. He'd been eight when his father had taken him to Mexico—a future pilot's first plane ride, a city kid's first trip beyond the bounds of the subway. All that brown Bronx slush forgotten the second they'd lifted off, winter gloom eclipsed by the thrill of flying. He'd known from the moment his toes sank into the warm sand that he was going to live somewhere like that. Just a shitty little seaside town, but the best his dad had been able to afford. All Will had known was that for the first time since his mother took off, the world had seemed beautiful again.

He wondered if Leigh had left some sad soul heartbroken in her wake. Will didn't think so. She was an actress, maybe a decent one, but even a guy as simple as Will could sense the pain behind the performance. He wasn't the type to pry or question, but he wanted answers from this stranger who'd managed to invite herself along on his evening. He was also a master of playing the free spirit himself, and if Leigh's front was anything like his, he wondered what burdens it was designed to hide.

He grabbed a fresh beer, dodged gyrating couples to make his way to Leigh and her dance partner. They were getting quite cozy, though surely not as cozy as Rex would prefer.

"Mind if I cut in?"

Rex departed with a shameless show of bowing and hand-kissing. Laughing, Leigh turned to Will. "You better deliver, Captain. He was good."

Will obeyed, moving in time with the music in his lazy fashion. "You might want to grab yourself some food before it's all gone."

She glanced at the grill. "I'm not hungry just yet. All I want is this." She stepped closer, and Will got distracted by the movement of her hips, the sheen of sweat along her throat in the firelight.

"You afraid of me?" she teased, noting his scrutiny.

"Only thing I'm afraid of is bats. I'm just trying to be professional, Miss Bailey."

She rolled her eyes and smiled. "Oh, right. My chaperone. Very professional when you wheedled that bribe out of me."

"I returned it, didn't I?"

"You did. And you can earn it back if you'll dance with me properly."

"What they call 'proper' dancing around this place will get you pregnant."

Leigh laughed again, a pure and thrilling sound. "Maybe not *properly* proper, then."

Will switched his bottle to his left hand and put his free palm to Leigh's waist, stepping closer, close enough for their knees and thighs to brush. From this near, she made him feel big in a primal, aggressive way he hadn't experienced in a long time.

She had that dancer build, a slender neck and long torso, proportions that seemed slightly improbable. Proportions women craved for themselves—the kind they respected, free of the more obvious curves that men's magazines sold like prime rib. Leigh moved as Will hadn't known American women could, as though no one was looking. As though she danced for the sheer physical pleasure the movement gave her. A supremely unprofessional thought had Will imagining what else her body might demand of his.

They edged ever closer. The drumbeat seemed to slow to the precise rhythm of sex itself. Will's thigh crept between hers, their hips separated by the barest of spaces. Her smooth hand settled on his ribs beneath his open shirt, her attention on his body as tangible as her touch.

He opened and closed his mouth, his fuzzy brain unable to supply one of the taunts that had so quickly come to characterize their rapport. Blood redistributed to dangerous places, and he strained to think of something boring. Something safe. Something to distract him from the curious, agile body brushing his.

As if someone upstairs had been misinformed that Will deserved a favor, the music wound down. The two of them stepped apart as the band disassembled for a break. Will and Leigh looked at one another, her pursed lips telling him she'd awoken from her little carnal trance. His collar somehow felt tight, despite all the buttons being undone.

"Thank you," she murmured.

"I do okay, as a partner?"

She nodded. "You did just fine. You're actually quite pleasant when you've got your mouth shut."

He shook his head and smiled. "Want some grub?"

"Sure."

He found Leigh a plate and she foraged at the grill. All the makeshift seats were taken, so they sat on the sand, off to the side with a view of both the ocean and the party.

"This is really lovely," Leigh said between bites. "Just what I needed."

"Good."

"I know you weren't supposed to let me hang out, so thank you."

Will shrugged. "I've never done what I'm supposed to.

Just par for the course." He studied her as she took in the scene. Her face had gone from pretty to sexy in the firelight, those grayish irises looking dark and liquid now, reflecting the flames.

"This must just be the same-old, same-old to you." She glanced at him suddenly, too quick for Will to pretend he hadn't been staring.

He cleared his throat. "I guess. But it's the same-old because we choose to do it nearly every night. Nothing much better I can imagine."

He looked at his friends of the last few years, his muscles melting with the easiness of this strip of sand. "In fact…" He trailed off, afraid of sharing too much with a stranger. She'd be the first he told, which felt far too familiar, far too soon.

She poked him with her elbow. "In fact what?"

Impulse had the words tumbling out before Will could stop them. "I, um… I'm going to buy a place on the mainland. In just a few weeks, I hope."

"Oh? You're going to move?"

"Eventually, yeah."

"But you'll still do all the flying out here?"

He shook his head. "No. I'm going to buy this run-down old vacation home, right on the beach. Sort of a shady part of town, but I'm looking to change that a bit."

"How?"

"I want to turn the place into a club."

"Like a bar?"

"Nothing fancy. Like this," he said, waving at the partygoers. "Bonfires on the beach, simple food, cold beer. Put in a patio for dancing, string twinkly lights everywhere."

"For locals only?"

"Nah, for everybody. Locals, tourists, runaway brides."

She smiled down at her plate.

"Just someplace to hang out. No pretense, no gimmicks."

"That sounds nice."

It did. And until last week it had seemed ages from real-ization, his father's doomed dream. The property Will could nearly afford to make an offer on, but to transform it into what he envisioned… Then after renovations there was staff to hire and train, licenses to procure, and of course the endless bribes that needed tendering to get the neighborhood's residents on his side. It'd take years on his stipend, and Will was even shorter on time than he was on cash. But with just a few innocent scraps of gossip sold to the tabloid, he'd be sitting pretty. He liked Leigh, though. He wouldn't share anything unflattering, and no photos. Still, the proposal sat heavily in his chest now, his golden opportunity having grown sharper and rustier barbs as he'd gotten to know this woman, uncertainty punching holes in his resolve.

"I'd like to see it sometime. Your club." Leigh's voice was airy, as though she was far away or half-asleep.

"It's not much to look at. Not yet. Just a tumbledown ruin on the beach."

"Do you ever visit it, and sit there and daydream, imagining what it'll be like? Like, 'hang a hammock between those two trees, a bar along there for people to set their drinks on'?"

Will felt himself blush, an unfamiliar sensation. "Yeah, I've done that."

"What will you call it?"

"Billy's."

"Is that your nickname?"

"No, it's my dad's."

"Oh. You guys are close?"

"We are. Close as you can be, living that far apart. He's been pretty sick, the last year or so."

"Oh, no. Like, cancer, or…?"

Will shook his head. "Armed robbery in his cab, shot in the stomach."

Leigh's hand flew to her lips. "Oh, my God."

"Three months before he'd planned to retire." All those years' careful savings, gone in a flash of gunfire. Will felt anger boiling in his gut, but kept his voice steady. "He was stuck in the hospital with infections for ages, and Jesus, it took a toll. He's sixty-two, but the last time I was home he looked about a hundred. I can shell out to see him and forfeit a week's pay here, or keep working and keep our necks above water on the medical bills."

A warm palm alighted on Will's knee, drawing him from his thoughts and back into his body.

"That sounds like an awful choice. I'm sorry."

He stared down at his hands. "Fingers crossed this unexpected gig I got offered will pan out, and solve some of those problems."

"Fingers crossed."

She felt close suddenly, and welcoming. Warm and soft as the fire's glow. It'd take so little to dip his face to hers. Such a tiny movement, yet such a huge nerve on Will's part, considering his arrangement. And even if his already questionable ethics took a hike, here was certainly not the place, not with all these witnesses.

Yet he could feel her inviting him, could see it in the way her gaze flicked from his eyes to his mouth to her hand on his knee. He could feel it as surely as he could feel his own body begging him to accept the invitation. There was something reckless and needy in her eyes, something that resonated inside him and brought his own impulsive, bad-idea desires to a steady boil. He wanted her, as badly as he could recall wanting any woman, the ache made deeper by his conflicted conscience and the impossibility of the setting. His brain felt fuzzy and he swallowed, his attention focused on her lips.

Loud laughter from the party woke him from the trance.

Realizing things were taking a sharp turn in a dangerous direction, Will sat up straight and cleared his throat. "So."

For a split second he saw disappointment tense her pretty face, then Leigh withdrew her hand, her tone turning light. "So?"

"Got it out of your system now? Bit of slumming to wash away that Hollywood glitz?"

"I'm not slumming."

"But you're going back. Back to your parties and premieres? You say you want to be a nobody, but come on. You'll miss that, right? Not today, but eventually."

"I've had my time to play dress-up and be the center of attention. Now I just want to be this, you know?" She stretched out her legs, digging her heels into the sand. "Just plain old me."

Will did the same, flexing his feet beside hers, intrigued by how small and pale hers were. "And so this is plain old you?"

"Yup. This is the most I've felt like myself in ages. Being around all these people who don't already have some idea about who I am, based on some character I played in a movie."

Will stole a glance at her profile, liking plain old Leigh. When they first met, he'd thought she must be a glutton for attention, to bail on her wedding day. Now he suspected it was more than that. Some awful mess she'd decided to tackle, not merely a dramatic near-miss with a silly, youth-clouded whim. Not a cowardly mad dash toward freedom and away from regrets and responsibility, as his mother's flight had been.

"What's your ex like?" Will asked. "What does he do, back in California?"

"He's a musician. Or was. When we met he was in a band."

"Rock star?"

She laughed, a weak sound. "Not quite. But his band was sort of an indie hit. They could go really far if they wanted, but he got bit by the Hollywood bug after we'd been together the first year. Now he's really ambitious about the scene, more than actual music. He was talking about producing. And he wants to open a club. Just like you." Leigh turned to stare at Will, her eyes narrowed with curiosity. "Actually, nothing like you."

"No?"

"He wanted to open a club, and make it the trendy new place to be. You sound like you want the opposite of that."

"Booze plus sand plus music," Will agreed. "Pretty basic formula."

"Sounds more my speed than what Dan wanted."

Dan.

"Sounds very nice," she added with a yawn. "I'll be sure to check it out when it opens."

"You do that. First round's on me." Actually, all her rounds ought to be on him, if his funding came through as he hoped. "You look bushed. You want me to walk you back to your place?"

Leigh frowned, but nodded. "I haven't gotten a decent night's sleep in days. But I'm sure I can find my way back by myself. The moon's nearly full."

Will stood, helping her to her feet. "Can't let guests wander around in the dark unchaperoned. I've broken enough rules for one night. I should at least pretend to be a decent escort."

They bade the hosts and guests a good night, and slipped into their sandals at the road. Will was in a sober enough state to drive her, but the walk would do him good. Clear his head, maybe screw it on straight about who this girl was to him. Maybe make an overdue phone call to his tabloid contact and start earning the money he'd been promised. What he'd sold his last few scruples for. Again, a sharp pain stabbed in his chest. But it had to be done, to avoid the far deeper heartache of failing his father. Will wasn't his mother.

He stopped at his place to ditch the cooler. He and Leigh

went barefoot again for the long stroll along the shore, sandals swinging from their fingers. The rising moon was indeed nearly full, casting its blue-white glow on the sand, across Leigh's face and the bare arms hugged over her chest.

"You cold?"

"I'm fine."

"Here." Will stopped and slipped his shirt off.

She smiled and accepted it, letting him hold her flip-flops as she buttoned it up her narrow frame, pulling her long hair from under the collar. Damn. What was it about a woman in a man's shirt?

"Thanks." She took her shoes back.

"Looking forward to another lazy day tomorrow?"

"Yeah. But first I need some real rest. I was so mixed up last night I just conked out on the couch. Now that I'm properly exhausted, eight hours' sleep in a real bed is my first priority."

"Big bed, too. One of those king-size football fields?"

"Yeah."

Will pictured such a bed, its gauzy curtains draped from a canopy carved from some endangered South American tree. Sleepy dawn sunlight, sleepy woman. Bare, slim legs wrapped in cool, slippery sheets—

Bad chaperone.

He combed his messy hair with his fingers and wondered for the first time in ages what someone thought of him. What did Leigh think of him? That he was lazy, probably. Enviably lazy, but lazy nonetheless. He had six years on her, but no doubt she was eons beyond him in making something of her life. Then again, he wanted no part of that twisted Western notion of what success was. He didn't want to wake up at sixty with any regrets. He didn't want to turn out like his old man, as much as Will loved him. And if that made him unambitious or a layabout or a scoundrel, so be it.

You could only ever hurt the people who relied on you—by leaving them, by your actions. The best solution was to keep relationships simple, responsibilities few and impersonal. Make no promises, suffer no regrets. If not for his father's tireless encouragement, Will never would have found the balls to move away and build his own life based on that motto. At first the guilt had eaten him alive, the shame of feeling he'd abandoned the only person he really, truly loved, and the one who'd sacrificed so Will could become whatever he dreamed of. That guilt had faded over the years, only to blaze vividly back to life when his father was shot. All those years Will had spent avoiding making ties, avoiding hurting anybody the way his mother had hurt him and his father… Here he was, a thousand miles away when his dad needed him most. All those good intentions, and he'd wound up the very thing he hated most—a deserter.

Now he had only one mission: to get his dad down here, to live out in paradise whatever time he had left. Will glanced at Leigh, hoping that perhaps her coming to him this evening might be a sign, proof that the deal he'd struck was meant to be, the right decision. He hadn't even had to go out of his way to seek her. She'd come to him.

Her villa appeared in the distance, moonlight glinting off its windows. All at once, Leigh stopped short in the sand.

Will scanned for danger, finding everything as it should be. "What?"

She took a huge breath, her chest rising, then falling as she let it go. She stared at her accommodations. "It's just so… empty. Especially looking at it from here. Like an aquarium or something. Like I might drown in there."

Will stared at the water and listened as she took another deep breath, then another. Then her small hand cupped his elbow.

When he turned to glance down at her, her face was at

once set and uncertain. There was a muted clap as her sandals dropped to the sand, his own sharp inhalation as her other hand went to his neck. Without thought he did as her touch commanded, leaning in to accept her mouth with his.

He tasted salt on her lips from the sea breeze. As he plunged the fingers of his free hand into her hair, she deepened the kiss. The rush of the waves seemed to fill his skull, drowning out all logic.

She didn't kiss the way she looked—not sweet, not inexperienced. No girl-next-door. She kissed with ferocity, making Will light-headed. The fingers stroking his bare skin curled, her short nails scraping, and self-control abandoned him.

Dropping to his knees, he pulled her down with him. A groan rose from his throat as he felt her weight, her thighs straddling his as he took her mouth. He tossed his shoes aside and pulled her close by her hips. Her tiny gasp warmed his mouth, and he angled his jaw to taste her. Words flashed across his mind—*rebound, tabloid, unforgivable assholery.* Abstract collections of letters, no match for the fascinating shapes of her body, the slide of her tongue against his.

He gathered her hair in his hands and took her deeper, suppressing a moan as her legs tensed around his, hips seeking friction. He gave her more than she asked for, tugging her hard against him, so close there'd be no mistaking that this lapse in judgment was mutual. She sucked her breath in sharply and went still in his arms.

He swallowed. "Now'd be the perfect time for one of your *wows,* Miss Bailey."

She bit her lip, not hiding her smile. "Call me Leigh."

"Call me Captain Burgess."

She shook her head, but her grin only deepened. There was something in her expression, something warm and easy that Will hadn't seen in years. He felt his loyalties growing foggy.

She cleared her throat. "I really shouldn't be on your lap."

"No, you really shouldn't. Especially since I'm so clearly trying to fight you off."

"This probably entails an exceedingly generous tip."

"Thirty percent." His heart wasn't in the teasing. It was in his throat, choking him, and in her hands, its resolve torn to shreds. It was also between his legs, blood pounding so hard he couldn't think straight.

She brought her face back to his. It became a far different kiss, deep and slow and hungry. It filled his head with smoke, his body with terrible, brilliant ideas. Leigh didn't protest as he cupped her breast. Her hips locked tight to his, moving in tiny thrusts that set his cock on fire. Curious hands stroked his chest, his stomach. Fingers flirted with the waist of his shorts and with a strangled moan Will managed to pull away, easy as gnawing off a limb. He relocated her hand to his side, catching his breath.

There was regret on Leigh's face as she fumbled to her feet. "Sorry."

"Don't be sorry." He stood, dusting sand from his shins.

"I'm… I didn't plan that."

"I'm sure you didn't. If you had, you'd have picked a far more deserving victim than me."

That brought a nervous smile to her lips.

"But you've been single for what? A couple days?"

"Yeah, basically." She bent for her sandals, not looking at him when she straightened.

"Hey, trust me, I'm flattered. But I'm sure you're feeling… Hell, I have no idea what you're feeling. But I don't want to be a part of anything you might want to take back, tomorrow or next week or when you land back in L.A." *Liar. It's your own regrets you're worried about.*

She nodded, still avoiding his eyes.

He went to touch her shoulder, but she dodged him, starting toward her villa. Will hurried after her. "Hey."

She stopped, unbuttoning the borrowed shirt and thrusting it at him. "Here. Thank you."

He tucked it under his arm, jogging to catch up. He grabbed her wrist and she finally turned to face him.

"I'm not angry or anything," he said. "I'm flattered beyond belief."

"You're trying to protect me, then?"

"I guess. But I bet you're going to tell me you don't need protecting."

Her mouth closed on its ready reply.

"I just don't want you to look at me the next time I fly you to the mainland, and see some impulsive regret standing there, overdue for a haircut."

She took a deep breath and released it as a sigh. "Did you want to kiss me?"

"You don't need me to tell you that. Did you want to kiss me? Or did you just want to kiss somebody who wasn't your ex?"

"I'm not sure." She stared at the sand. "I think I wanted to make a mistake. I've spent ten years terrified of screwing up, and you…you have nothing to do with my life back home. I guess you seemed like the right person to finally screw up with."

Will rubbed his hands over the bumps rising along her arms, then draped the shirt around her shoulders. "Why'd you run away, Leigh? Did he bore you, or hurt you?"

She didn't reply.

"Fine. It's none of my business. And I'm not such an upstanding guy that I'm hurt by the idea of being somebody's reckless rebound."

Leigh shook her head, her smile full of annoyance.

"But some withered little chivalry gland in me's screaming that I need to jump in that ocean and cool off. And for some reason I'm going to listen to it."

Leigh nodded. "Your gland is probably wise."

"So you okay? You gonna be able to get a lift to Bridgetown from me without flinching?"

"We'll see. I'm sure you could find a way to make me flinch regardless." She smiled again, this time looking sheepish and soft. "You know, you're a nicer man than you give yourself credit for."

And you're an adorable, wonderful fool to think it, and far too kind for the likes of me. "You're the first person who's ever suggested that, but go ahead. Enjoy that delusion. Feel free to log it in the guest book."

She looked toward her lodgings. "Walk me to my door?"

They crossed the sand in silence, and Will followed her up the steps to her patio, past the pool to the sliding doors. He spotted her bed through the glass and quickly looked elsewhere.

Leigh fished her key card from her shorts. With a tap, the lock beeped and a tiny light turned green with approval. She met Will's eyes. "Thank you."

"No problem."

"I promise I won't come bugging you again, asking for stuff that's not listed in the brochure."

"My loss."

She stood on her tiptoes and touched his shoulder, kissed his jaw. As she pulled away she made her posture ramrod straight and offered him a curt, hyperprofessional salute. "Good night, Captain Burgess."

He returned the gesture, then slipped his hands into his pockets. "Sleep well, Leigh. And sleep in."

She slid the door open and waved as she closed it, then disappeared into the darkness of her suite.

By the time he descended the patio steps to the beach, Will was shaking. Tiny tremors, from the adrenaline. Lust and surprise and guilt all poured in a blender and zapped into a cocktail that would knock any rational man on his ass. He rubbed at a knot forming in his chest, and aimed himself home, gulping deep breaths until his heartbeat slowed.

As he rounded the curve of the shore, he slipped his phone from his pocket, checking the time.

Late, but not too late. And no matter the hour, there was a phone call that needed making, to a man back in L.A. who'd pay good money to hear what Will had to report about Leigh Bailey.

5

"IT'S NOT A HURRICANE, is it?" Leigh watched the two maintenance workers folding her lounge chairs two days later at lunchtime, stowing stray furniture in a storage bay set into the patio. She'd been awakened by a call that morning saying the staff would be by to secure things ahead of an approaching storm.

"No," one of them said, fastening the canvas cover on her hot tub. "But very windy. You'll be fine. Just don' want these things flying all 'round when it get gusty. But no need to panic. Should be over by tomorrow mornin'."

"That's good."

"An' these villas are built like rocks, miss. Best you stay indoors, of course."

She pictured the cottages perched on stilts at the workers' beach and wondered how well they would fare.

She thanked the men when they finished the preparations, feeling excited about the coming storm. She hadn't made any plans for the day, had no activities she'd been hoping to try out. Staying inside with a glass of wine in her hand and watching the sea thrash sounded lovely. Simple and lovely. And it'd keep her away from Will Burgess for another day, which was surely for the best. Leigh shook her head, lamenting what a fool she'd made of herself that second evening. She'd blush pink as a grapefruit the next time she needed a lift to shore.

Just as she was finishing dinner, the winds arrived. She noticed it in the ocean first, a quickening of the waves lapping the beach, a rising of the tide. Then the sky grew heavy with fast-moving clouds, gleaming gray as gunmetal.

Leigh settled on the couch with a glass of chardonnay to watch nature's show. No commercials, no gossip, no reminders of the mess she'd left back home. Simple, elemental. Not unlike those few passionate minutes in the sand with Will. She gave herself a little mental shake for remembering it with such idiotic fondness. She was just another rich, bored tourist to him, surely, some laughable caricature of the jet set. It had stung to realize those facts, the morning after their... collision. Though the embarrassment didn't do much to take the edge off the giddiness still wriggling in her middle. Her actions had been foolish, but her crush was as real as ever.

By seven it was dark as midnight, with wind and sea spray whipping the villa's picture windows. There hadn't been any lightning, but Leigh's skin felt fevery, her senses heightened as though something electric charged the air. She rose to go to the fridge, and as she refilled her glass, a great crash shattered her calm, and the bottle slipped from her hands, exploding across the tile. She whipped around to find one of the solarium's tall panes all but obliterated, wind and spray gusting in to send the magazines and papers on the coffee table flying. She tiptoed around the bottle shards and hurried to the phone by the door to dial zero.

"Reception," chimed a friendly islander voice.

"This is Leigh Bailey, in Shearwater Villa. I think something just crashed through my living room window. There's wind coming in and stuff flying everywhere."

"Will you be all right for ten minutes, miss?"

"Yes."

"Please shut yourself in a different room and collect anything you'll need for an overnight stay. I'm sending a car right now, and we'll get you to a room here in the main complex."

"Thank you."

They hung up and Leigh picked her way along the edge of the living room, collecting her phone from the table and her sandals from the floor beside it. She could see what had happened; lying amid the solarium glass was a heavy terracotta roof tile.

Her ride arrived before she had finished tossing a change of clothes into a bag. To her surprise, it was Will, standing on her stoop with his messy hair whipping around his face, his truck parked behind him. He looked comforting and familiar, solid in the midst of the chaos. Her middle gave a funny wriggle.

She had to nearly yell to be heard over the gusting. "Hello again, Captain." She shut the door at her back and Will took her bag.

"What happened?"

"A roof tile got blown through one of the windows. What are you doing here?"

"I was the only one left in the vicinity, still battening down my hatches after I got the plane secured." He opened Leigh's side of the truck, the courtesy seeming surreal in such violent weather. She climbed inside and he joined her shortly in the cab.

"Where are the other workers?" she asked.

"I suspect the slumber party's already begun," he said, starting the engine. "This happens a few times a year. The workers' village is on the quietest inlet, but they still evacuate us, set us up with cots and amenities in the main complex, around the pool. But don't worry. You'll be treated very well." His tone was warm, but a touch false. He sounded as though he was speaking to any old guest, not the one whose body he'd held tight two nights before. She missed the real Will, the shameless one, and worried she'd scared him away.

"Sorry about the inconvenience," he added politely as he got them onto the road.

She found the balls to turn and stare until he met her eyes during a straight stretch. "I sort of liked you better when you were a jerk, Captain."

Will faced forward and his smile arrived slowly, lit by the light of dashboard gauges. "Apologies. What about the other night? Is that off-limits or do I get to harangue you for trying to take advantage of me?"

She relaxed, pleased she hadn't ruined their rapport. "Just don't treat me like some delicate visitor flower. That's all I ask."

"Never been sexually assaulted by a guest before," Will said, facing forward. "Just trying to be polite, lest you manhandle me again."

"Womanhandle, you mean."

Another grin.

"You can get away with a lot," Leigh said, "since you're the only man who can get me off this island."

"If we're being indiscreet again, I'm going to go ahead and delete the last two words of that sentence."

She replayed her remark and rolled her eyes at him. "That sounds more like the Will Burgess I know."

"First class, all the way."

"Indeed."

"But never fear, we shan't cross paths tonight. You'll be put up in the emergency suite, away from us commoners."

"Emergency suite?"

"It's nicer than it sounds. It's on hand to placate guests when there's a malfunction, or if they're feeling ill and need to be near the medical staff. Or most often, if their marriage breaks down and the husband gets the boot from the love nest. The workers call it 'the doghouse.'"

"Oh dear."

Will steered around a trash bin that had been blown into the road. "Doghouse or not, it's lovely. You'll be spoiled rotten. They always bend over backward when anything goes wrong."

"I don't need spoiling. Just shelter."

They lapsed into silence for the rest of the trip, and Will got them safely to the parking lot outside the reception building. "I'd hold an umbrella for you, but I'd rather not get swept out to sea." He opened his door and pulled her case from behind the seat. Leigh saved him the trouble of opening her side, and hurried behind him through the punishing wind and into the warm, dry calm of the lobby.

The manager hurried forward with a broad smile. "So sorry about this, Miss Bailey."

Leigh smoothed her wind-whipped hair and offered a smile of her own. "I don't mind. I just hope the room isn't wrecked."

"Shall I show her the temporary suite?" Will asked. He took the key card and led her to the left, past the fountain.

"If there's anything you need," the manager called after them.

"I'll ring, thank you," Leigh said.

"No charge!"

Will showed her up a flight of stairs and down a hall to a beautiful suite that overlooked the dock and *The Passport*. It was nowhere near as spacious as her villa, but just as tastefully decorated, hardly an afterthought. She wondered exactly how often this space did get used for the crises Will had mentioned, both medical and marital.

He set her suitcase beside a desk.

"Thanks."

"You're very welcome." He paused before adding, "Sorry this trip's not going quite according to plan."

She shrugged. "When does anything ever go according to plan? Or if it does, what fun is it, anyhow?"

He grinned at that, the last of his formality melting away to reveal the man she'd developed a speed-crush on during that party. "Well put."

Leigh glanced at her feet, vaguely noting that her shoes were plastered with wet sand. "While I have the chance, I want to apologize for the other night. For being such a freak when you were nice enough to walk me back."

"Already forgotten about it."

She knew it was a fib, meant to lessen her embarrassment, but she couldn't help but feel a bit sad. She wouldn't be forgetting *his* kisses anytime soon. "It's been a weird time for me. I lost track of my head. And I could have gotten you in trouble for it, so I'm sorry."

His smile turned tight, his expression melancholy. "I don't want your apology, Leigh. And I don't need it. I shouldn't have lost my mind right back."

"At least you found yours."

"Barely… But if anyone was suspicious about my walking you home, my going missing with you now won't help matters."

"True."

"I'll leave you to get settled in. Milk that free room service for all it's worth."

He headed for the hall and they exchanged sheepish waves.

She felt better as the door closed behind him. Good to know their romantic collision seemed to have left Will feeling foolish, too. At least that meant it had gone both ways, not just her throwing herself at him, some deluded crazy woman.

Crap, she really ought to have tipped him, just now. She'd have to *over*tip him the next time she flew to the mainland, take a page out of his book and hide a crumpled bill in the plane's cabin.

Still, Leigh couldn't settle down. The formerly fascinating storm had lost its appeal the second it sent that tile smashing through her window, and the gusts rattling the panes here were far from soothing. Flipping channels only made it worse, as her old anxiety over stumbling across gossip about herself churned her stomach. She wished she had a jar of peanut butter.

She checked the room service menu, but nothing fit the bill. She didn't want something fancy delivered on a silver platter. Maybe there was a vending machine downstairs, with candy bars or cookies. She dug her wallet from her purse and pocketed her key card.

The building was bustling, the staff rushing around to get displaced workers set up with cots and food and towels.

Leigh was cast cursory, anxious smiles as she wandered around the ground floor. She walked through a large rear recreation area, with a big pool, a sauna, deck chairs. A place for people to congregate, she guessed, if they were renting the villas as part of a destination wedding or other well-heeled occasion. She recognized faces from the barbecue among the workers getting themselves set up with clusters of cots. People were delivering blankets and pillows, looking as though this was no new drill. Only Rex, the shameless flirt she'd danced with, paid her any special attention, though he was too preoccupied to offer her much more than a mischievous glance. Will strode past, a heavy jug of bottled water hugged to his chest and a package of paper cups tucked under one arm. Oscar and Bethany were there as well, Bethany rubbing her huge belly as her husband set up cots for the two of them, sleeping pads for their children. Leigh frowned. She wandered over, mission forgotten.

"Hello again, miss." The woman wore a cooler, more professional smile now than she had while manning the grill. "Heard your villa had a little mishap."

"It's no big deal. They set me up in the emergency suite."

"Is everything all right?"

"Oh, it's fine. But I can't help but wonder if maybe you'd like to swap with me for the night?" She nodded toward her belly. "I can't imagine a cot's going to be comfortable for you."

"Don't you worry about me," Bethany said with a wave. "Don't be silly."

Leigh didn't think she was being silly, she thought she was being logical. But she realized now that maybe her idea would've gotten the woman in trouble, so she didn't push it.

"It's a very kind offer," Bethany said. "Very kind. Thank you. But I'll be jus' fine."

Will reappeared with a blanket in his hands, which he tossed onto a cot not far from the couple. "Looking to crash another party?" he teased.

"I was just asking if Bethany wanted to switch with me for the night."

"Ah."

"'Course I said no." She shook her head. "Sweet of you," she added to Leigh.

"Very sweet," Will agreed, and he gave Leigh a calculating glance.

She didn't know what to make of that look, so she changed the subject. "Is there a vending machine anywhere?"

"Sure. It's called room service."

"I don't need room service, not when all this is going on. I just wanted a candy bar or something." Something distracting and decadent, though now that she was close to Will once more, his distracting and decadent kisses sprang vividly to mind, eclipsing her sugar craving.

"Never mind. I'm not actually hungry." She felt dumb. Her

naive offer had clearly made Bethany and Oscar uncomfortable, and now Will thought she was even sillier than before, totally out of touch with the guest-worker dynamic, some ridiculous cartoon of a dippy Hollywood actress. She bade them a good night with burning cheeks.

WILL WATCHED LEIGH WALK away, more confused than ever. But one thing was for sure—he'd made the right decision after their passionate mishap on the beach, backing out of that deal with the tabloid bottom-feeder. The second he'd told that asshole where to shove his money, it was as though Will had finally remembered how to take a deep breath.

Obscene paycheck or not, she wasn't some generic celebrity to him anymore. She was kind and lost and vulnerable, and she didn't deserve to be spied on, much less be written about by an opportunistic creep. Will had called the editor, planning to tell him a few harmless facts, but had wound up cussing the guy out. So much for a quick fix to his money problems. So much for pretending he didn't have an ethical bone in his body.

Someone else might've seen Leigh's kind offer to Oscar and Bethany as obliviousness, but Will found it charming. She was so lousy at being privileged that she didn't automatically view herself as an "other," an outsider, a guest. It was downright adorable and deserved rewarding.

Once his cot was set up, he headed for the kitchen. It was chaos, with the cooks throwing meals together for workers and families who hadn't had supper yet. Will slipped through the bustling crowd and headed for the pantry, poking around until he found a selection of American candy bars. They kept them stocked, along with a variety of offerings from the U.K., for the inevitable requests from homesick guests. Will picked three, hoping one might prove a favorite of Leigh's.

He was no stranger to the inside of the emergency suite—

he'd escorted motion-sick guests there more times than he could count. He hid the candy behind his back and knocked on the door. Leigh answered shortly, dressed in a bathrobe.

"Hello, Captain."

"Hope I didn't wake you."

"Not even close." She opened the robe, revealing the shorts and top she'd been wearing earlier. "Just chilly. What can I do for you?"

He arranged the candy bars in a fan, and her laugh warmed his entire body.

"Are you my vending machine?"

"I am."

She eyed the choices. "That was awfully nice of you."

"So was your offer to Bethany, asking if she'd like to swap rooms."

Leigh picked a Snickers bar, holding it in both hands as though he'd presented her with a rose. "That was really dumb, wasn't it? My thinking it was even an option. She'd probably get in trouble." Will could tell from Leigh's face that she was more than embarrassed—she was disappointed.

"Not dumb. Kindness is never dumb. Just a bit naive."

She smiled and fiddled with the candy wrapper, letting him see how dopey she felt. "You must think I'm completely out of touch."

"I think you're lovely," he said honestly, careful to keep all flirtation from his tone. With the guilt of his deal gone, it was too tempting, being close to her like this. Being close to her mouth, her hands, a bed… He fought his body's every carnal instinct and took a step back.

She shrugged and held the Snickers up. "Thanks for this."

"It's nothing. Don't look so bummed. No one thinks any less of you, naive or not."

"Oh, I'm not worried about that. Not really. I *am* bummed

that she can't have the room, though. She's got to be close to nine months pregnant."

Will nodded. "She's due this week, I think."

Leigh sighed in frustration. "It's ridiculous for me to get that huge bed all to myself."

Don't think about the huge bed. Don't think about the huge bed. "If she gets uncomfortable she can sleep in the infirmary. It's nothing fancy, but it'll beat a cot."

"I guess that's something." Leigh glanced around the room. "I'd invite you in to hang out, but that's probably naive of me, too."

"Probably." But awfully tempting.

Sadness passed over her pretty face, dark as a shadow.

"You okay?"

She nodded. "Yeah."

It occurred to him then, that she was lonely. His libido cooled. That was why she'd crashed the party, and hit on him, and why she looked so lost in this beautiful suite. She probably had swarms of people hounding her day and night back home, and this trip hadn't been planned with solitude in mind.

But it wasn't his concern. Will had fraternized enough as it was, and hanging out with Leigh—romantically or only as friends—wasn't good for either of them. Dangerous for him and his job; bad for her, surely, as she worked to wrap her head around the dissolution of her would-be marriage. Plus he still felt like a shit for ever having agreed to report on her vacation to that tabloid. Damn guilt. He'd been right to avoid feeling the emotion for so long, keeping his life free of promises and regrets. It felt terribly heavy, like a ball and chain.

"Hope you sleep well," he said, taking a couple more steps toward the door.

"You, too. Thanks again."

Will smiled and set the extra candy bars on the table beside the door, earning himself a sheepish grin. She thanked him again and they said good-night, and a sense of safety, of dodged bullets, encased him as he closed the door.

LEIGH AWOKE TO THE heart-stopping sound of human wails.

She shot up straight in her jumble of blankets, and the clock told her it was just past midnight. She pulled on the robe, grabbed her phone and hurried out into the hall in her bare feet. Voices came from down the stairs, female sobs and gasps, low male rumblings. Fear stiffened Leigh's muscles but she ran down the steps.

"Hello?" she called.

The voices ceased, as though the speakers feared they'd been caught. She turned the corner and found Oscar and Bethany standing there in their pajamas. Will appeared from the lobby, a middle-aged woman right behind him.

"Her labor's started," Oscar said to Leigh, by way of explanation and apology.

"So sorry to disturb you," Bethany added with a wince.

"Don't be ridiculous. I was just worried someone had been hurt."

The woman Will had fetched must have been a doctor or nurse, since he stood aside to let her and Oscar help Bethany waddle into a side room.

"Oh my," Leigh said to Will.

"She'll be fine. She's been through this drill twice already."

"God, what a time to go into labor."

He gave her a warm but tired smile. "Saved someone a stressful drive, having it happen here."

"That's true. Are their kids awake?"

He nodded, then stifled a yawn. "They're being looked after."

Suddenly exhausted herself, Leigh took a seat on the carpeted steps to the second floor. "There's probably nothing I can do to help, huh?"

Will shook his head. He gave her another of his searching looks.

"What?"

"It's making you nuts, isn't it? Not feeling useful."

"A little."

"Come with me."

Intrigued, she followed him back to the pool area. He checked that the kids were behaving for the woman who was now trying to get them resettled, then headed for the spot where Oscar and Bethany had been sleeping. He handed Leigh a paperback and a bottle of water, and poked around, finding a cell phone and a pair of pink flip-flops. They walked back to the infirmary and Will knocked on the door. "Everybody decent?"

"Yes," the nurse called.

They entered the clean, small room. Bethany was propped up on a hospital bed, her husband holding her hand while she cradled her belly. She was breathing deeper than before, the panic gone from her voice. She thanked Will and Leigh as they set the salvaged items on a cart by the bed.

"It'll be a long labor," the nurse announced. "Contractions are very far apart still."

Leigh looked around, thinking poor Oscar could use a chair, but not knowing where to find one.

"How long?" Will asked.

"If I was a betting woman, I'd say eight hours, at least," said the nurse.

"They should take Leigh's room," Will stated firmly.

Bethany shot him a look as though he'd suggested Leigh birth the baby for her.

"Come on," Will argued. "You can hobble around, watch TV, get comfortable. If the kids get antsy, they can camp on the couches. Leigh doesn't mind."

"No," she said. "I really don't mind at all."

"I'm not telling management," Will added. "Would you guys?"

The couple and the nurse exchanged glances.

"I didn't think so," Will said. "So come on. I'll get Leigh set up someplace discreet, and when you realize what a great idea it is, shuffle on up there and take it easy. Okay?"

Oscar frowned, but his wife gave him a beseeching glance. "Maybe," he allowed.

"Well, take it or don't, but it's at your disposal." Will turned to Leigh. "Come on."

As they headed up the stairs to her suite, she murmured, "You did that for me, more than her."

He smiled at her as she swiped the door lock. "Maybe. Do you wish I hadn't?"

"God, no. What kind of jerk would hog this room when there's a woman downstairs looking forward to a night of labor in the middle of a storm?"

Will waited as she reassembled her suitcase, and they left the key card on the floor outside the door.

"Lemme think where we can put you where management won't stumble over you in the morning and wonder why you're not in your assigned room."

"What about a steam room or something?"

"That could do. If you're not claustrophobic."

"Nope."

"Sauna it is. I'll find you a pad and some blankets and pillows."

Will dropped her at the room in question, down a short hall from the pool, and returned with the promised amenities. It was a unisex sauna, meant for people to use wearing swimsuits, and a skinny window in the door precluded privacy. But there were two levels of wide cedar benches along three walls, a perfectly adequate space for a sleeping pad.

"This'll be just fine."

Will's lips opened and closed, seeming to hold in a thought. He took a seat on the far bench.

"Yes?"

"You're really nice, offering Bethany and Oscar your room after your own villa got wrecked."

"You were awfully nice, bullying them into accepting the offer. I won't get anyone in trouble over this, right?"

He shook his head. "We watch each other's backs. And I'll watch yours."

"Good."

He pursed his lips.

"What?"

"You're lonely, aren't you?"

She thought about it, realizing the answer with unexpected clarity. "I am. Or at least, I don't know how to feel comfortable being alone anymore. Must make me look a bit pathetic."

"Not at all. Just explains why you lost your mind and deigned to make a move on me the other night."

Leigh blushed, glad it was likely undetectable in the dim light. "No, that wasn't why. I wanted to."

"Was I just the nearest available man for the job?"

She shook her head. "No. You just… It felt right. You seemed right, at the moment. You seemed like everything I wish I had, personified. Freedom and simplicity."

"I am simple, that's true."

She smirked. "You know what I mean. So no, you weren't just convenient. You did something to me." And he still did. The steam room felt suddenly small and impossibly quiet, intimate, away from the howling squall outside.

"You did something to me, too," Will said softly.

She fought to downplay the pleasure his words gave her. "Yes. It was called sexual assault."

He cracked a smile, but sincerity radiated from his gaze. "I wanted what you did, so don't feel like you made a fool of yourself. If we'd met under other circumstances, I wouldn't have stomped on the brakes. Trust me."

There had been a fist around her heart, and she felt its fingers relax, all the regret she'd been carrying around pumped cleanly away in a few beats. In its wake she felt the other emotion it had been shrouding—affection toward this man. More than mere affection. *If we'd met under other circumstances,* her mind echoed. If they had, she'd shuffle her butt along this bench and kiss him again. If. As it was, anyone could walk by and catch them, and get Will reprimanded or worse.

"Would you have asked me out, under other circumstances?"

He laughed and shook his head. "Not in any world where you're a movie star. Your entourage wouldn't have let a bum like me near you."

"Maybe in these other circumstances, I'm just some normal girl. A waitress or something."

"A waitress," he murmured, pondering mightily. "Yeah, I'd ask you out as a waitress."

"Oh, good."

"I'd have tipped you outrageously, as well."

"That'd be a role reversal."

Another laugh, a rich rumble that made Leigh feel as though someone must have switched on the steam. Her crush was back, worse than ever. Damn the room's hateful window. In need of a distraction, she ripped the candy bar open and took a bite.

"Now you'll never get back to sleep," Will said.

She shrugged. "My body's still got no clue what time zone I'm in. You want some?" She held out the Snickers.

Will scooted down the bench and stole a bite. They swapped the bar back and forth in silence for a few moments, and Leigh struggled to keep her mind off how close his thigh was to hers, and how warm it must feel through his khaki shorts. She'd felt that heat for herself, his firm muscle, his needy kiss. She'd smelled his skin, its scent mingled with salt water and the tropical, fertile smell of the very island, floating on the breeze. She raised her chin and met his eyes in the ambient light.

"What were you like, back in New York City?"

The question stumped him a moment. "Young. I left before I was twenty."

"But, you know… Were you the same as you are now, personality-wise?"

He shook his head. "I was irritable and impatient. I was a New Yorker. But I knew I wasn't where I was supposed to be. I was like a parrot in a cage. I'd been born in that cage, but I still knew it wasn't where I belonged."

"I wish I knew where *I* belong."

"You knew enough to get out of the wrong marriage. Plenty of people don't realize that until it's too late."

"Have you ever been married?" Leigh asked.

He laughed softly. "No, not even close."

The answer made her melancholy. She had no more than a silly crush on Will, but the commitmentphobia implicit in his reply still disappointed her. Yet how could this man be any other way? Any romance beyond a one-night stand must weigh him down like a threat of grounding rather than the promise of steadiness, of stability. Leigh wished she could adopt a similar philosophy. In the wake of Dan's betrayal, its simplicity had an appeal… But she wasn't wired that way, for better or worse.

"What?" he asked, after her silent scrutiny had gone on for some time.

"Nothing. Just wishing I was more like you. Better at being…adrift, I guess."

He nodded. "Requires a very special set of lazy genes, to be as careless as me."

"It doesn't look careless, being you. It looks liberating."

"No one's life is quite how they lead you to believe. Freedom comes with its own burdens."

"Like what?"

"Lots of questions, lots of wondering if you ought to regret your choices. Guilt about leaving people behind, to put yourself at the center of your universe."

She considered that. Her own universe was out of whack. Leigh felt trapped at the center of her parents' harried orbits, trying desperately to adjust to everyone else's gravity field, lest she fly off into space.

"Is it ever lonely, being your own sun?" she asked Will.

He paused thoughtfully. "It is and it isn't. I've got the company of more friends and visitors than I can count, out here. But there's only one person in the world I really love, and I left him behind."

"Your dad?"

He nodded. "It was the price I chose to pay, the cost of living in a way that felt right for me. It's a steep one, though. I know I'm missing out, not keeping my family close, not making room for a wife or kids."

"Maybe you'll settle down someday."

"Maybe."

She pictured such a thing. Imagined Will and a faceless wife, a couple faceless kids, him tethered in a home and a city, his energy crushed by responsibilities. Regrets. She imagined herself then, with an older version of Dan, her own faceless children. Would she have swapped the peanut butter jar for a wineglass? A prescription bottle? She prayed not, but then again, it was such a very common fate for women in her position. Was she really so special that she could presume herself above it?

Leigh sighed heavily and set the candy bar aside, arranging her pillows and lying down with her head a few feet from

Will's hip. She stared up at the ceiling. "How on earth did people of our grandparents' generation settle down straight out of high school? How did they make these decisions so young, and see them through?"

"Not everyone does. See their commitments through, that is," he added, his voice flat.

"I guess."

"It was different back then. Adulthood began practically at adolescence. Now it starts somewhere in the early thirties, as best I can tell. Which reminds me—I really ought to grow up soon."

She smiled at that.

"But you must know all about being a grown-up," Will said. "You got discovered at, what, seventeen?"

"Yeah, but I didn't come into my own or anything. I've done nothing but take other people's advice for the last ten years. If I even still have some internal compass, I doubt I'd know how to read it, it's been shut in a drawer for so long."

"I'm sure it's fine. Just take it out and give it some exercise."

"I tried that. And I wound up throwing myself at you."

"See? There you go. Your intuition's bursting with genius ideas."

"That's not what you said before. You said I must be nuts, picking you over a more 'deserving' man, or something like that."

"I was just being kind, to make you feel better."

"Uh-huh."

"Look, Leigh…" He trailed off with a heavy breath. "Nobody knows what they're doing. Not the most powerful CEO on the planet, not the president, or your parents. Not you, and definitely not me. Don't worry if your life doesn't feel as tidy and resolved as some movie character's, just before things fade to black. Because it won't. You're breathing, which is all it takes to be doing things right, from day to day."

"Your low standards aren't without their appeal."

He leaned over to smirk down at her. "Neither are yours," he said, clearly meaning her romantic standards of late.

She stared up at his handsome face, that bone-melting smile. Their shared gaze lingered longer than was platonic, and she wished he'd lean down and kiss her, window be damned. Instead he reached over and swept her hair from her face, gently finger-combing it into order. His attention had drifted from her eyes to her throat or chin, and she watched him swallow.

"I better let you get some sleep," he said.

"You, too," she agreed, though the last thing she wanted was for him to leave her side. "I hope your plane's okay out there."

"She will be," Will said, getting to his feet. "She's seen far worse than this. Anything else you need, madame guest?"

Leigh shook her head. "No, I'll be okay."

"I'm sure you will." He opened the door to the steam room and murmured a discreet, "Sleep well, Leigh."

"Good night, Will."

6

LEIGH WOKE IN UTTER confusion, scrambling to remember where the heck she was. It came back in a flash and her body relaxed, then tensed all over again as she wondered how poor Bethany was faring with her labor. A knock on the sauna door cut off her fretful thoughts, and she found Will's face framed in the window, his eyes shut.

"I'm decent," she called, sitting up, tossing aside the blanket and knotting the robe. She rubbed her tight back as Will slipped inside.

"Sleep okay?" he asked.

"Not bad. I wish Bethany could say the same."

"I went to see them early this morning. They used your suite, then the labor really kicked in and Bethany was moved back to the infirmary."

Leigh breathed easier to hear their scheme had gone off without a hitch. "And the baby?"

"Still taking its sweet time."

"Speaking of time..." Leigh found her phone under the pillow. "Nine o'clock. My goodness."

"The storm's just about over. I already went to check and make sure my meal ticket still has both her wings. Most everyone's already eaten, so forgive me for running off, but I'm starving and the workers' breakfast will be over soon."

"Can I join you?"

Will's expression turned hesitant.

"It'd be more fun than going up and ordering room service and eating by myself."

"The staff will wonder why you're eating with the workers."

"Let them. Let them think I'm a dimwit who wandered in thinking it was a buffet." Leigh slipped on her sandals and tidied her hair. "We all just survived a wind storm. I'm sure they've got plenty of things to worry about besides one misplaced guest."

Will relented. "Fine. You slept on a bench last night, after all. Guess you've earned some indulging."

He gathered her bedclothes and slipped outside, leaning against the door and blocking the window while she dressed. He gave her a signal when the coast was clear. Leigh and her bag exited without detection, and Will led the way back to the pool area. A buffet station was set up against one wall, only a few workers still eating off their laps on lounge furniture and sleeping pads. Oscar and Bethany's kids were back. Their babysitter was beside them, reading a book, but they were conked out. The little girl had fallen asleep with her feet dangling in the pool, her normally noisy mouth slack and silent. Her older brother was curled into a snoring ball.

Leigh and Will fetched food and sat on deck chairs, facing the pool's calm blue water. She had to laugh, not just at the kids, but at everything.

He shot her a curious smile. "What?"

"Just my honeymoon. That I slept in a steam room, and here I am eating breakfast on a deck chair with you."

"Can't blame the storm or your fiancé on those two particular facts," he said.

"Ex-fiancé. And no, I wasn't blaming anyone. Just thinking, this is the first time in ages I've been calling the shots for myself, and look where I've chosen to be."

His smile deepened. "Either your taste reflects really well on me, or my company reflects rather poorly on you."

She gave him a long, searching look. He could pretend to be a scoundrel all he liked, but having spoken to him so intimately the night before, Leigh didn't buy it. Maybe Will really did have a low opinion of himself, or maybe he just favored the image, but she could see through it now.

A worker hurried in from the front of the complex, dodging scattered chairs and blankets and clutter, to rouse the children. Leigh caught the words *a little girl,* and smiled to herself as the kids shoved their feet into flip-flops and were hurried off to the infirmary to meet their new sister. Leigh turned to find Will also smiling.

"God help the parents if she's as much trouble as Ninna," he said, shaking his head.

"How exciting," Leigh replied.

"You want kids?"

She nodded. "Someday. Not for a while, though. Not until I know what the heck I'm doing with my life. But yeah, I think so. You?"

Will looked thoughtful. "I'm not sure. I've never been with a woman where I could picture it. Picture any kind of grown-up, permanent future, I mean."

Another pang, another reminder that Will wasn't built for long hauls. Silly thing to feel let down by, but it tightened Leigh's chest nonetheless. Rebound crushes weren't nearly as simple as she'd been led to believe. This one had her downright mixed up, in the head and heart.

They finished their breakfast and sat in easy silence for quite a while, until the nurse came striding in, grinning when she caught sight of them.

"You want to meet the island's newest resident?" she asked quietly as she reached them. "They wanted to invite you both."

Leigh sat up straight, looking hopefully at Will.

He shrugged. "What's one more breach of visitor-worker separation?"

They followed the woman back to the infirmary. The kids had gone, but Oscar was lounging in a chair beside the bed, Bethany propped up, the baby bundled in her arms. She wore a wide, exhausted smile.

Leigh and Will came close to stare down at the adorably pissed-off-looking infant, her eyes scrunched closed, head dusted with fine black hair. Leigh couldn't help herself when a gooey "awww" tumbled from her lips. She hadn't seen a baby so new since her little brother had been born, when she was five. It tugged at something in her middle, something that said *Yes, let's make one of these someday.* Bad timing, considering she'd ended the most serious relationship of her life five days earlier. *Someday,* she agreed nonetheless. *Someday not at all soon.*

"Have you named her?" she asked the couple.

"Sesane," Oscar said proudly.

"She's beautiful. Congratulations."

"Thank you," Bethany said. "And thanks so much for your generosity last night."

"Yes," Oscar said. "Was a long labor. *Long* labor. It was so nice for Bethany to be able to watch television, get her mind off things."

"It was my pleasure," Leigh said.

"We better leave you three to rest," Will said, reaching down to smooth the baby's wispy hair. "She's gorgeous. Congratulations."

"God save us all if she takes after her sister," Oscar said.

Will laughed. "My thoughts exactly."

They said their goodbyes and left, closing the door quietly behind them.

"I better head to the cove and see how the settlement's held up," Will said. "I hope they get your window fixed soon, so you're not stranded too long."

Leigh shrugged. "I'll cope." She was dying to volunteer to help, but she couldn't follow Will around any more than she already had, couldn't continue to foist herself on the workers like a motherless duckling. "Thanks for letting me impose."

"The pleasure was all mine," he said, and though his tone was lofty his words seemed sincere.

Leigh remembered that voice in the silence and dark of the steam room, the things he'd told her and the closeness she'd felt. She ached to ask him to hang out again sometime, invite him to continue the small bond they'd found in the dark, and the sexual connection that had sparked between them beside the lapping waves, under the stars. But she knew she'd asked too much of Will already. It was his risk to take. He'd be blind not to know she felt something, and if he felt the same, it was his turn to make it known.

"Maybe I'll see you again sometime?" It was a question, not a statement, the invitation implicit. She held her breath, waiting for his reply.

All he did was nod and say, "Guess I'll see you whenever you decide to visit the mainland."

Disappointment cooled her body like a dunk in ice water. "Guess so."

And she watched him stroll away, taking a little piece of her heart with him.

WALKING AWAY FROM LEIGH and her invitation was about as easy as tossing oneself bodily into a volcano.

Will couldn't give a damn about the minor risk to his own professional reputation if they hung out again. Other workers had crossed lines with visitors in the years he'd been employed by the resort, and few had been ratted out, even fewer reprimanded—only the ones who'd been complained about by regretful guests in the wake of their impulsive choices. He doubted Leigh would do such a thing to him. So no, it wasn't job security he was worried about. But after what he'd nearly done to her, selling information to the tabloid, he knew in his heart he didn't deserve what she was offering him, be it sex or romance or mere companionship.

Though he wanted it, badly.

Thank goodness they'd been in the lobby when the invitation had come up. There he'd stood a chance of denying her. Had they been alone when she'd aimed that heated glance his way… He swallowed, his body warming at the mere thought. He just had to pray they could avoid one another until it was time for her to fly to L.A., out of his life and back to the world she'd surely come to miss once the novelty of paradise wore off.

He kept himself busy with minor repairs to people's homes, all the time tugged by the memory of what had happened on the short stretch of beach between where he stood and where Leigh would be, once her villa was habitable again. She'd be so close.…

He worked until he was too tired to be tempted, relieved that flights would resume the following day and keep him far away from her.

But the very next afternoon, Will's resolve was tested. As *The Passport* splashed down beside Harrier Key for the final time that day—with Leigh's recovered luggage on board and in need of delivery—he promised himself he'd be good. He'd be professional. He'd be courteous.

And he'd be praying to God the entire time that he wouldn't give in and do anything stupid.

LEIGH OPENED HER DOOR just as the sun was sinking, expecting last-minute maintenance people. They'd been in and out all day, finishing repairs to her solarium window and roof. She was shocked to find Will there instead. Shocked, hopeful, nervous, thrilled…

"I come bearing gifts," he announced, holding up the suitcase that had gone missing back in New York.

"Oh, wow." She stared uncertainly at the familiar bag. Inside were her clothes, physical reminders of her life back home. Her favorite shampoo and all the memories its fragrance would trigger, underwear bought with Dan in mind. Her phone charger would ruin her lame excuse for not checking her messages and returning frantic calls. No more need to conserve her battery. Though the bandages had to be ripped off sooner or later.

Will set the case on the stoop. "Guess they got your window all patched up."

"They did. Everything okay back in the cove?"

"Yup. Nothing we couldn't tackle with an afternoon's effort, thank goodness."

She studied him where he stood, that casual stance, casual clothes, easy smile. But something else, too. The same edginess she felt. A reckless thought had words tumbling from Leigh's lips.

"So you're all done flying for the day?"

"I am."

"Would you like to hang out? Maybe see if there's a Knicks game on or anything?" When he didn't answer right away, she got desperate. "I'll buy you dinner."

His expression was hard to read, eyes squinting with some cagey emotion or other. She'd thought they were friends now, after the way they'd talked in the steam room, but maybe she'd dreamed it all. Blown it out of proportion.

She sighed, feeling dumb. "Sorry. I know it's inappropriate to even ask."

He laughed. "Jesus Christ, Leigh. Quit apologizing. Impropriety doesn't bother me. Just give me a hard sell and I'll decide if I'm more intrigued by a chance to watch the game than I am scared of us arousing anyone's suspicions, hanging out yet again."

She smiled at that, relieved and hopeful. "Okay. Well, the fridge is full of beer and wine, and I'll order you whatever you'd like to eat, no matter how overpriced. I just don't feel like being alone with myself. You're free to go whenever you want."

He nodded slowly. "Okay. But I'm paying for my own dinner, and I'm dropping my truck off first. I don't need the others spotting it and suspecting I'm here giving you some other kind of room service."

"Good thinking."

"But I'll be back."

He waved as he climbed into his truck, and Leigh went inside. She spent the next hour killing time, just long enough to change her clothes and empty her rescued suitcase, and to begin worrying Will wouldn't be back. But a knock from the rear of the villa brought a grin to her lips. She jogged up to her room and slid the door aside as Will kicked his sandals off on the patio. And just like that, Will Burgess was in her bedroom. A fresh flush warmed her face, seeming to trickle down her neck to heat her chest, her belly, lower. *Mercy.*

Cool yourself, Bailey. "Come on in. I checked the Knicks schedule, and you're in luck. They're playing at seven."

He rubbed his palms together. "Excellent. It's been ages since I've caught a game."

Leigh led him through to the open living room. "You're extra lucky, since I was going to have the service cancelled. But then the storm happened and I forgot."

"Cancelled? Why?"

"I can't be trusted to not go looking for stuff about myself."

Will grinned. "Finally, the infamous Hollywood narcissism reveals itself."

"It's not narcissism. Well, maybe it is. But it feels more like paranoia. Like you're at a big party and you walk past a room and hear people talking about you. I think it'd be hard for anyone to resist eavesdropping, whether they're being praised or ripped apart."

"Or lied about."

She gestured that he should have a seat. Will crossed his legs and stretched his arms along the back of the couch, looking perfectly at home both in his jeans and T-shirt and the villa's luxurious surroundings.

"The lies are annoying," she agreed, "but it hurts way worse to get cut down just for being yourself. I mean, everybody else goes to the corner store in their pajama bottoms once in a while. They don't get critiqued for it."

"I hate to break it to you, but you're in the wrong business."

She smiled. "That's not news. Can I get you a drink?"

"Beer would be great."

She examined the impressive stock in her fridge and chose a microbrew for Will, uncorked a bottle of white wine for herself. She set their drinks on the coffee table and took a seat in an easy chair, worried that sitting on the couch might suggest she was trying to get them cozy again. Which she wouldn't mind, frankly, but given the chaos in her head at the moment, it was most certainly a bad idea. Plus Will was the one who'd be at risk if they took things too far. It ought to be his lousy decision to make, his move.

She desperately hoped he'd make it.

They tapped their glasses together and drank. Will scanned the space. "I've never been inside this unit before. Except that morning when I fixed your coffeemaker."

"Really?"

"Barring the random mishap when I get recruited to help deliver some drunk visitor back into the arms of their temperate spouse, there's no reason for me to be inside any of the villas. It's nice."

Leigh glanced around appreciatively. "Yeah, it's gorgeous."

"Better be, for that price tag."

"I shelled out for privacy, not decor."

He nodded, looking away, at the windows or the beach beyond.

The game wasn't on for another hour, but Leigh grabbed the remote, finding a pregame report and keeping the volume low. Loud enough to fill any potential awkward pauses, but soft enough to allow conversation.

She fetched the dinner menu from the counter. They passed it back and forth, and Leigh called in their orders. She returned to the lounge and folded her legs beneath her butt, leaning into the chair's plump armrest. Will was distracted by highlights from a previous match. Leigh let silence reign for a long time, enjoying the easiness of sharing this space with her companion. And just like at that party she'd crashed, the calm came from Will, not her environment. She ought to get a prescription for him, in pill form. *Pilotrex,* she named her invention. *To soothe jangled actresses. Take with alcohol.*

Eventually she aimed a smile his way, waiting for him to turn. When he did she said, "I'm glad you came over."

He shrugged. "I've had no better offers this evening. Thanks for inviting me."

"You're welcome." She sipped her drink, a wicked thought popping into her head. "So you've really never been in here before? No other female guests have ever lured you into their villas?"

He laughed. "No. They've tried, though."

"Yeah?"

"The resort does its share of over-the-top weddings, so I have been set upon by the odd bridesmaid."

"Or the odd bride."

"Yes, very odd," Will agreed, his evil grin making it clear he knew the bride she was implying. "If it makes you feel special, you've gotten further with me than any other guest."

"That does make me feel special. And surprised. Seven years you've worked here, and you've never had a fling with a guest? Do you have some kind of ethical code or something?"

He shook his head. "You've bribed me—what do you think? But the kinds of women who stoop to solicit the help, they're usually either drunk or repressed, or a bit of both. I'm a cad and all, but I won't sleep with a drunk woman unless she's my girlfriend. And I won't chance sleeping with anyone I think will regret it the next day, since they can report me and get me fired. And I like this job. And, you know, I like being able to sleep at night. That's tough to do when you think a woman's making a mistake with you."

A mistake. Exactly what Leigh had wanted—she'd even told him as much. "So that's why you, you know…put the brakes on things that night after the cookout? Because you thought I'd complain to the management about you? Do I seem that unbalanced?"

"Well, no. I won't pretend it's just self-preservation. I meant what I said. I just didn't want you to leave here regretting anything you did with me. Why? Exactly how much did I miss out on?"

She laughed and stared down at the wine in her glass.

"Third base?"

She held her tongue and sipped her drink.

"Further than *third?* Something that'd have us finding sand in awkward places for the next week?"

Leigh grabbed the throw pillow wedged between her hip

and the armrest, and whipped it at him. Will laughed, holding his bottle out of harm's way.

"Why me, then?" she asked, the wine making her a touch shameless. "How come I managed to get further with you than any of the other hot-blooded resort ladies?"

"Well, you're unnaturally good-looking. Let's not discount that."

The comment brought a blush to her chest and neck. It went beyond mere flattery to something she craved deeply— being praised for her looks by someone who'd seen her with no makeup, no styling, no facade. Being told she was pretty just as she was.

"What else?" She was definitely flirting now, but it felt nice. It felt better than nice—it felt *normal*.

"Your hips are rather…persuasive."

"Even though I got no ass?" she asked, quoting Oscar and Bethany's loudmouthed daughter.

Will faked propriety, his gaze drifting innocently to the ceiling as he sipped his beer. "I haven't looked, so I couldn't say."

"Sure."

"Why? You check mine out yet?"

She grinned. "Not intentionally. But you do spend a lot of time walking in front of me."

"Classy, Bailey. Very classy."

She drained her glass and got up to refresh it, bringing Will another beer.

"You're trying to get me drunk," he said as he accepted the bottle. "You slip something in this?"

"I'm just being a good hostess, Captain." She paused before brazenly adding, "I promise I'll never make another move on you. That ball is in your court."

Will's blue eyes stayed glued to her face, but his open mouth made no sound. When he did look away, his gaze settled on the king-size pillow propped at the other end of the couch. "You said your first night here, you slept on the couch."

"Yes. And the second and third."

"Something wrong with your bed?"

"It's too big."

"Too empty," Will added, his sad tone telling her it wasn't a flirtation.

"I'll give it a shot tonight, though. Maybe."

"He really did a number on you, didn't he?"

The question landed like a slap, but Leigh kept a firm grip on her emotions this time. "I won't go into it. But it's hard when any relationship is over, no matter who got dumped or who did the dumping. Whether it's a romance or a friendship or anything else."

"How long were you guys together?"

Leigh laughed, frustrated. "You really aren't attracted to me, are you? Because you're definitely not gunning to make that move I offered you."

"No, I'm definitely attracted to you. I'm just hopeless with women."

"I believe it. Well, Dan and I were together just over two years, since you asked. What about you? What was your longest relationship?"

"Year and a half, I think."

"Here in Barbados?"

He nodded, and Leigh wondered what she'd been like, if she still lived in the Caribbean, if she was a local or a transplant or some vacationer he'd seduced into an extended layover.

"She got bored with me," Will added with a shrug. "Left me for a boat captain." He made a face that told her such a thing was tantamount to murder.

"You don't sound too brokenhearted."

"I value mobility. Romance is great, but it's a bit of an anchor."

Leigh bit her lip.

"What?"

"Nothing."

"You've got that look that usually tells me I've offended somebody, so go ahead, let me have it. I've probably earned it."

She frowned. "It's just that I used to think that, too, about my ex. That he was like my anchor. But meaning that he kept me grounded. Not that he held me back."

Will seemed to ponder their disparate definitions as he sipped his beer. "Guess I just don't care much for feeling grounded," he concluded.

"Probably a good instinct for a pilot." Funny how it made her feel inexplicably sad, though. "But I don't know how to steer myself very well. Without an anchor I feel like I'm just blowing around in the wind, like I could end up any—"

The doorbell chimed.

"I better duck behind something." Will hopped up and headed for the bathroom.

She answered the door and the delivery woman carried two covered trays to the counter. Leigh bade her a good night. The food smelled heavenly, leaving Leigh instantly ravenous.

"It's safe to come out, Captain. Dinner is served." She set each lid aside with a clank. "The front desk must think I'm a binge eater."

Will met her in the kitchen and they gathered cutlery and plates and napkins.

They ate in near silence, watching the pregame coverage, Leigh joining him on the couch. She marveled again at how comfortable she felt in his company. Perhaps nothing so simple as friendship, but not far off. It felt as it had with Dan, in the early days. Natural. And "natural" was a scarce commodity in Leigh's world.

Will made short work of his pasta, while Leigh picked listlessly at her fancy salad. Stupid salads. She must have been issued some requisite Hollywood mind control injection shortly after her move to L.A., one that caused women to only ever consume lettuce when witnesses were present.

"Not enjoying your dinner?" Will asked.

She shuttled arugula around with her fork. "It's fine, but I'm not sure why I ordered it. Wish I'd gotten comfort food."

"Like mashed potatoes and stuffing?"

"Like peanut butter."

"Peanut butter?"

She nodded. "Right out of the jar."

He looked amused. Then the game started and Leigh felt Will's attention leave her. She didn't mind it in the least; it was relaxing to feel ignored in this casual, companionable way. She glanced at his thigh, half a cushion from hers. She wished she could scoot over a foot and feel his hip pressed to hers, warm and comforting, deepening the evening's pleasant ambience. She wished other things—things to do with Will's lap—but pushed the ideas away lest she go feral on him again. She really needed a distraction from this distraction.

She was fidgeting, tapping her plate with her fork. When the first ad came on, and Will gave her a look. "Peanut butter, huh?"

"Yup."

"That's all it takes for you?"

"I'm easy."

He was on his feet a moment later.

Leigh shifted onto her knees to lean over the back of the couch, watching him trot up the steps to her kitchen. "What are you doing?"

"Answering your prayers, I hope." He began rooting

around in her cupboards, then her pantry. "Ah, jackpot." He hauled a white plastic bin from a high shelf and set it on the counter. Leigh jogged over to inspect it.

"Every suite's got emergency staples, in case of storms." The box was full of canned soup, nuts and dried fruit, and a gorgeous sight indeed—peanut butter.

"Oh, my God, you're wonderful. I take back all those things I said about your manners when we first met." She grabbed the jar and a spoon and headed back to the couch, mouth watering.

Leigh stretched her legs out between them; lounging was essential for proper peanut butter abuse. Her salivary glands tingled as she unscrewed the cap and peeled off the safety seal, stirred to blend in the oil. She breathed it in as another woman might savor fresh lavender.

Will glanced toward her.

"Ignore me," Leigh said, coating the back of the spoon.

"Smooth or crunchy?"

"Smooth."

"That work for you?"

"Oh, God, yeah. Smooth is the best. Duh."

"Obviously," Will agreed, watching as she wallowed in the first taste.

"And this is the good stuff. Not that awful frosting-type peanut butter, with sugar and shortening in it. 'Ingredients,'" she read off the label. "'Roasted peanuts, salt.'"

"You're quite the connoisseur."

"It's my favorite vice."

"You going to eat that whole jar?"

She shook her head. "Maybe half."

Will laughed and turned back to the game. "Whatever works for you."

"Beats a drug habit."

Another laugh, one that warmed her middle. "I'm going to fly you to Miami and check you into peanut butter rehab."

Leigh shot him a horrified look and hugged the jar to her chest. "Never. I'd rather die in a gutter with the spoon still in my mouth. You should have seen me when I first discovered Nutella. Now *that* was a bender. Can't be trusted with that stuff."

"Here." Will made a "gimme" motion and Leigh loaded the spoon and handed it over. She tried her level best not to make it sexual, watching him share her utensil, her ridiculous sin. He nodded his approval and handed it back. "I can see the appeal."

"Yeah?"

"Sure. Plus when I was in high school my dad quit smoking, and to replace the cigarettes he took to eating lollipops. He went through a retail-size tub of them every month."

Leigh smiled at the thought of a hardened New York cabbie driving around with a Tootsie Pop stem jutting from his lips.

"Never weaned himself off them, actually," Will said. "Replaced one unhealthy habit with another. But I'd rather he rot his teeth than his lungs, so no complaints."

"I'm glad I never took that up. Smoking."

"Me, too. Beer's enough for me. Booze and sunshine."

"You'll have even more of those once you get your bar going."

Will nodded slowly, turning to the TV. He seemed distracted, but not by the action on the screen, Leigh didn't think. One of the Knicks sank a three-pointer and his expression didn't change a jot. After an outlandish foul against New York failed to rouse Will from his trance, she began to fear he might be upset about something, maybe caught up in worries about his dad's medical issues. Then—

"You feel like a walk?" He looked at her squarely.

"A walk?"

"Just along the beach. I'm not really watching this." He nodded to the television. "Not that I don't appreciate the invitation. But I could use some air."

"Sure."

When he stood, Leigh set her jar and spoon aside and followed, feeling nervous. They exited through the bedroom, stepping into the cool evening breeze. They crossed the patio and strolled to the shore, the lapping water sounding intimate and secretive after the color and ruckus of the game. Will cuffed his jeans and waded up to his knees, Leigh to her ankles. She enjoyed the feeling of the current and the fine sand, the suction tugging at her feet with each retreating wave. That comforting sensation of being anchored.

"You okay?" she finally asked Will.

He turned, sliding his hands into his pockets. That gesture meant something, she was coming to realize, some imitation of casual calm when he was feeling the opposite. How strange that she could know this about him after only a few days' acquaintance. How strange and pleasurable.

"I'm fine."

"That means less than nothing in man-language."

He smiled at that. "You annoy me, Leigh."

She blinked, the remark knocking her off balance. "Oh?"

"Yeah. I want you to be this one way, and you keep proving yourself to be some other way."

"What way do you want me to be?"

In the low light leaking from the villa, his smile tightened. "I guess I want you to be what I expected—a bit more spoiled. Or shallow."

She relaxed. "Sorry. I don't see why that annoys you, though. Spoiled and shallow sound far more irritating to me."

"It's annoying because I like things in my life to be simple. It makes them complicated when people aren't what you expect."

Dan's face sprang immediately to mind.

"It's annoying because if you weren't so sweet and charming and weird, I wouldn't be stuck struggling this hard to not find you attractive."

She pursed her lips, the comment making her feel floaty, held down only by the drag of the sand at her ankles. "Oh."

Will stared off to the side, at the dark water. "It's much easier to play two-dimensional pilot to your two-dimensional tourist."

"Instead of what? Friends in 3-D?"

He nodded, still not meeting her eyes. There was a struggle being waged inside him, between his dick and his professional conscience, she guessed, or perhaps between his dick and his aversion to complicated women. In either case, his dick seemed likely to be involved, which had Leigh's hopes up in an instant, along with her pulse.

"Have I inflamed your chivalry gland again?"

A tiny laugh huffed from his nose and Will met her gaze. "Something like that."

"Could just be a peanut allergy. Which would be tragic. Though it'd leave more for me, I suppose."

His chest rose and fell with a deep breath; his eyes studied the water between them. Whatever his conflict was, it must be intense, to render this shameless man so uncertain.

"Are you trying to think up reasons not to make a move on me?" she asked quietly.

"No. I've already got a very legitimate reason not to do that."

"What? Job safety?"

"Just my reasons."

She frowned. "Have you got a girlfriend?"

"No, of course not."

"Is it because I'm on the rebound?"

"Not really, no."

Leigh took a stab at levity. "I hope it's nothing to do with my hygiene."

At long last, a smile. "Definitely not."

"Then can I make a suggestion, Captain Burgess?"

Will nodded. "Sure."

"Don't overthink it. As long as you're single, I don't mind you making a move on me. I don't have any expectations of you, except when it comes to getting me to the mainland. Everything else that might happen, it's just between us."

"Right."

"And I'm going to go out on a limb and suggest that, unlike me, you're not especially good at overanalyzing things. You look pretty constipated."

He laughed.

"So do me a favor and quit trying to figure me out. I can't stand being theorized about any more than you could probably stand being...stuck in a traffic jam."

"Try hospital waiting room."

"Or that. But whatever we might have, it'd just be a fling, right? Flings aren't meant to be thought about too deeply. Flings and peanut butter are two of life's simplest pleasures." She grinned hopefully at him, though she knew in her heart a so-called fling with Will Burgess wouldn't be simple. There'd be a fresh, bitter taste of heartbreak when it was over, but it was a price she was willing to pay to explore their connection. A pittance.

"You're a very decadent woman," Will murmured, barely audible over the waves. He slid his hands from his pockets and beckoned to her with a curled finger. "Come here."

As Leigh stepped closer, he stepped back. A pace for a pace, and by the time she reached him the water was at his hips, her navel. Strong hands, assured once more, cupped her shoulders, spreading warmth through her entire body.

"Whatever this is," he said, "it has nothing to do with anything else we might be to each other, right?"

Her heart tightened a little at the caveat, but that was okay. She had a crush on him, so it was only natural to feel a little twinge. It would fade soon enough. "I know the score. This is whatever it is."

Will nodded, his expression softening. He kneaded her shoulders, lips parting. So strange that he could take her up into the sky without a moment's hesitation, yet this kiss gave him such obvious pause. Leigh angled her face and he took the hint, lowering his mouth to hers. The water was cool around her legs, Will's lips hot against hers. Everything about him felt like this place; leisure in the soft scrape of his stubble, luxury in the easy way his mouth took hers. He'd seemed like a man who'd kiss the way he spoke—bluntly and without caution— but he was far more sensual. His kiss felt new, all the excitement of a teenage fling with none of the sloppy inexperience. Leigh's first kiss had been staged, a scene from her breakout movie, but if she'd had a real first kiss, this should have been it. She wrapped her arms around his neck and surrendered.

His fingertips slid along her collarbone and up her neck, his hands clasped her jaw. She melted, letting him take her mouth deeper. She raked her fingers through his hair and a moan rumbled from his throat, humming through her body.

His hands skimmed all the way down her back to her hips, her thighs. He tugged her up and Leigh wrapped her legs around his waist, their bodies separated by too many wet layers for her liking.

The kissing turned shallow, a distracted sweep on their lips as the action drifted southward. Held in place by his strong hands on her butt, she shifted against him. She felt him as she had the second night, hard behind his fly.

Wrapping her hands around his arms, she imagined his muscles flexing and straining as he braced himself above her in bed. In *her* bed, a mere minute's walk from here. In her bed back home, this new and thrilling man desanctifying a once-exclusive space. The thought ought to trigger anger or regret, but she felt only lust, hot and simple, tightening her body, tightening her legs around his hips. She didn't want him for who he wasn't—not-her-ex—or as a palate cleanser, a rebound. She wanted him for exactly who he was, a notion that put her on edge with danger as much as excitement. She could fall for him, easily. But he need never know. Let him still believe this was about making mistakes.

The hands holding her urged her closer, stroking their bodies together in time with the waves. The ridge of his trapped erection was rubbing her just where she liked, the friction making her hungrier with each motion. His harsh breaths warmed her lips and she imagined other sounds, equally rhythmic and desperate.

Leigh pulled away enough to peel her shirt up her torso and fling it toward the shore for the waves to deliver. She'd put on a bikini while she'd been waiting for him earlier, thinking if he stood her up she'd wallow in the whirlpool. She certainly hadn't been picturing this, though it was a far nicer use of her swimsuit. He held her against him with a single hand, the other stroking her back, passing over the bow securing her top, one pluck from taking them to the next level.

She felt his hips moving, felt gravity intrude as he walked them to shore. He made it to his knees and lowered her back onto the wet sand, waves lapping her legs. In the far too dim light, she watched Will strip away his shirt, and thank goodness she didn't have to pretend she wasn't ogling him for a change. Whatever the many projects were that filled his free time and gave him this body, she approved.

As he lowered himself, she didn't waste a moment. Her legs wrapped around his waist and she welcomed his weight, the thrilling press of his hard cock despite their damnable

GET FREE BOOKS and FREE GIFTS WHEN YOU PLAY THE...

Just scratch off the silver box with a coin. Then check below to see the gifts you get!

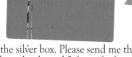

SLOT MACHINE GAME!

YES!
I have scratched off the silver box. Please send me the 2 free Harlequin® Blaze™ books and 2 free gifts for which I qualify. I understand I am under no obligation to purchase any books, as explained on the back of this card.

151/351 HDL FV7T

FIRST NAME	LAST NAME

ADDRESS

APT.#	CITY

STATE/PROV.	ZIP/POSTAL CODE

Worth TWO FREE BOOKS plus 2 FREE Mystery Gifts!

Worth TWO FREE BOOKS!

Worth ONE FREE BOOK!

TRY AGAIN!

Visit us at: www.ReaderService.com

HB-L7-01/13

DETACH AND MAIL CARD TODAY!

HB-L7-01/13

© 2012 HARLEQUIN ENTERPRISES LIMITED
Printed in the U.S.A. ® and ™ are trademarks owned and used by the trademark owner and/or its licensee.

If offer card is missing write to: Harlequin Reader Service, P.O. Box 1867, Buffalo NY 14240-1867 or visit www.ReaderService.com

BH-17-10/13

BUSINESS REPLY MAIL
FIRST-CLASS MAIL   PERMIT NO. 717   BUFFALO, NY

POSTAGE WILL BE PAID BY ADDRESSEE

HARLEQUIN READER SERVICE
PO BOX 1867
BUFFALO NY 14240-9952

NO POSTAGE
NECESSARY
IF MAILED
IN THE
UNITED STATES

clothes. He slid his forearms into the sand beneath her back so their chests brushed, drawing the breath from her lungs just as his mouth claimed hers once more. He thrust his arousal against her, the motion a cruel tease. The need grew maddening, until she finally pushed his shoulder and he shifted to her side.

"Too many clothes," Leigh said, fumbling with the snap of her shorts.

Will watched as she flung the garment aside. He promptly returned the favor, standing to wrestle off his drenched jeans and kick them away. Beneath were cotton boxer briefs, soaked from the sea, leaving little to Leigh's capable imagination. Above the waistband, a trail of fine hair blazed a path from his navel, across abs dotted with water from the surf and dusted with sand from the beach.

She wanted him for who he was, beyond a mere rebound or fling. For the way he looked at her now, a man staring at a near-naked woman, Leigh's celebrity a nonentity, as far from this beach as her old life felt.

She came closer on her knees, enjoying how tall he seemed, standing before her. His gaze followed her hands as they surveyed his calves and thighs, the groove of hard muscle at his hip. A sharp breath rewarded her when she stroked his stomach, and his next words were strained.

"You remember my chivalry gland?"

She met his eyes, palms sliding south to graze his thighs. "I do."

"It's fallen out. So don't count on me to stop you doing anything you might regret."

She smiled, lowering her gaze to his belly. "The only thing I'd regret tomorrow is holding back tonight."

She sensed Will nodding, then a thrill trickled down her spine as his palm alighted on her head. He pushed her hair back, tucking it behind her ear. Leigh traced the bulge in his shorts with her thumbs, slow and taunting.

A groan was her warning before his fingers closed over hers, drawing them over his shrouded cock, holding it tight. *Wow.* Harder than she'd ever felt a man get, thicker than she'd ever hoped for. Her legs went wobbly as she let him guide her caresses, stroking her palm up and down his length. He'd been many ways with her—galling, kind, brusque, uncertain—but the commanding feel of his hand on hers…this was the only way Leigh wanted him to be from now on.

With her free hand, she toyed with his waistband, easing it low to expose the crease where his thigh met his trunk, and his damp, soft hair. His bossy hand let hers go, and together they drew his briefs down. His cock was warm and smooth against her palm, his smell faint and fascinating. Again, she felt the weight of his palm on her head, cradling. She memorized him with slow strokes, a dozen or more before she put her lips to his flesh.

His moan gave her chills, offset by the fever of his intimate skin. She tasted the sea first, then Will's own flavor in its wake. She wanted to be amazing for him, to hum and whimper and spoil him with mind-blowing tricks she frankly didn't possess. But worse than that she wanted to please him, she wanted to be herself, so she did her best and hoped her enthusiasm made up for her lack of technique.

He let her find her pace, then met that rhythm with tiny thrusts. Leigh felt high, from his size in her mouth, his sounds, the heat of his base wrapped in her hand. The fingers in her hair trembled as his stomach clenched, all the cues of his body telling her he'd gone from aroused to crazed. She told him with her actions that she was in this to the end, but with a gentle motion, he drew her hand away and eased himself from between her lips.

His chest rose and fell, then he swallowed deeply before meeting her eyes.

She could feel it coming—an apology, an excuse that would let him leave her here, kneeling in the sand like a fool. But none came, merely a lust-drunk smile as he pulled his briefs back up and crouched before her, taking her hands.

"You got a bed in there?" he asked, nodding to her villa.

"You know I do."

"Never been slept in?"

She shook her head.

"That's a terrible waste."

"Agreed."

Will grinned. "Let's give the housekeepers something to gossip about."

7

THEY DUMPED THEIR WET clothes on a patio chair, and Leigh's heart sped as she glanced at the bedspread through the sliding glass doors. Everything about this moment felt exotic—the soft pile of the carpet under her bare feet, the scent of the flowers on her dresser. Even the moon was in on it, a perfect circle of white slanting its glow through the huge windows. Will began to slide the door shut, but she stopped him.

"I want to hear the ocean."

He pushed it back open with a smile. "Want to wash away some of this sand and salt?"

Leigh could have been tarred and feathered and it wouldn't have slowed her down, but she nodded, leading him to the bathroom.

"Damn." He scanned the room, the floor-to-ceiling glass cubicle of the slate-tiled shower, the elegantly rustic bowl-style sinks and spotless mirror, the sunken whirlpool tub in the corner. The tub was tempting, candles at the ready, but Leigh didn't protest when he went to the shower instead—standing or lounging, she'd take him naked and wet in any context he liked. She studied the exquisite flex of his back muscles as he fussed with the taps.

He held out a hand. "Ladies first."

Leigh kept her bikini on and stepped into the stall. Hot water rinsed the salt and sand from her skin and hair, cool stone soothing her feet. Will joined her, closing the door. They stared at each other, a pause full of appreciation and awe.

He laughed. "Jesus, you're sexy."

Leigh grinned. "Thanks." She scanned his chest and stomach, scarcely daring to believe this man was hers to enjoy for the evening. "And I didn't invite you in for your conversational charms, so that compliment goes both ways."

"Cute." He stepped closer, cupping his broad hands over her hips, eyes feasting.

Leigh's eyes had already had their fill, however, and her fingers wanted their turn. She grabbed the soap and twirled it around and around until suds dripped from her hands. She started at his throat, slipping to his chest, lingering on his abs. Another gorgeous groan as she stroked lather over his bulge. She was especially thorough at the task, marveling as he grew for her again, the weight and stiffness of his cock in her slick hold promising too many delights to contemplate.

"Here." Will took the bar from her. He backed her gently against the rough stone wall, casting her in his shadow, as exciting as having his body above hers in the sand.

"How tall are you?"

"My license claims I'm one hundred eight-five centimeters," Will said officiously.

The conversion was beyond her, but he was six feet, at least—far taller than the average actor or musician in Leigh's experience, and she added this to the growing list of Will's superior traits.

"Why?"

"I'm just objectifying you." She glanced at another exemplary part of his body, hidden by his underwear.

"How'm I doing?"

"You're fantastic. How am I doing?"

He smiled, hands still busy with the soap, making her impatient. "I told you before, you're unnaturally attractive. Shall I send a note to your personal trainer?"

"I don't have one."

"Must be your dancer genes, then."

"Must be." Her mind went fuzzy as he touched her—soapy hands gliding up her arms, lathering the nape of her neck, her collarbone and finally her breasts. As he leaned close, his erection brushed her belly, his mouth settling against her temple. He kneaded and teased, driving her wild until he reached around to untie her suit. As the top slipped from her shoulders, the way his lips parted was the greatest compliment she'd ever received.

She shut her eyes and gave in to this marvelous sensation, of this man worshipping her body. His hands slid lower, lower still, then he was on his knees before her, planting kisses on her belly and hips. Her bikini bottoms had pointless ties on either side, but rather than tug it down, he set the soap aside and took the time to free each knot, her final scrap of modesty falling away and taking her sanity with it. She ground her shoulders against the slate, knowing this was the same soft scrape he felt beneath his knees. His knees—this tall, shameless man, kneeling at her feet. Goddamn.

She raked her fingertips through his wet hair. His hands roamed up and down her thighs, flirting with her curls but still making her wait. She clutched his hair in her fist, just rough enough to assert her impatience.

Will kissed her hip bone. "If you think I'm going to rush this, you're insane."

"And you're mean."

A haughty hum punctuated his grin. Slippery fingers traced the insides of her thighs and she stepped her feet wider. For what felt like ages, his touch edged closer, closer, only to back off. She tightened her fist, begging. At long last, the pad of his finger glanced her clit, making every muscle in her body tense.

His tongue traced the corner of his mouth.

"I saw that, Captain Smug."

He smiled up at her. As he stroked the seam of her lips, Leigh gasped, melting against the wall. His touch was slow and deliberate, delicate enough to keep the pleasure maddening. She let his hair go, cupping the back of his neck.

Will put his mouth to her hip, his eyes closing as his fingers slid inside her. Holding his face close, she wished to feel his mouth other places, but this shower was a logistical issue. Will added a third finger and she reveled in the sexy, explicit feeling of his penetration. When the pleasure became all at once too much and not nearly enough, she pushed him away and bade him stand.

"Bed."

"Bed," he agreed. Arousal had his lids looking heavy, his lips parted, and Leigh wanted to watch a hundred other emotions pass over that face, preferably as he stared down at her from above.

They rinsed away the suds and toweled off in record time, Will finally kicking his shorts aside. He made it to the huge bed first, stripping down the comforter to expose satin sheets, some dark color indistinguishable in the moonlight. He climbed atop them, just about yanking Leigh with him. She settled on top of him, his erection pinned between her legs. She'd been poised to savor, but his bossy hands took hold of her hips, drawing her forward, easing her back. Hard, thick, hot—exactly how this man ought to feel. He was a fling to wreck all others, the best Caribbean souvenir a greedy woman couldn't buy. Will felt like far more than that, frankly, but she couldn't let the crush take too strong a hold.

"On top of me," she muttered, moving to the side.

He obeyed in a flash, kneeling between her legs.

"Tonight," she began.

"Yes?"

"Not all the way. Not yet."

"Whatever you ask." He took his dick in hand and swept his head across her slick folds and clit. Wondrous.

For a minute or two she luxuriated in the sight and pleasure, then the ache in her belly demanded more. But they were moving so fast. Too fast. There were condoms in her bathroom cabinet, fancy ones wrapped in gold foil that she'd first mistaken for chocolate coins. But no. She was here for two weeks. They ought to save something for later…if there was a *later,* a *next time.* Regardless, there was plenty to explore tonight without rushing to the finale.

He brought his body alongside hers and drew her thigh over his. More of that maddening ache as he stroked his stiff length against her sex, her wetness turning the drag of his skin to gliding friction. He grunted softly with each push, only deepening how badly she wanted to feel him inside her. Still, the caress was heaven—perfect pleasure as he slid against her clit, a pure and agonizing tease as hot as penetration itself.

"Will."

His hand on her lower back felt possessive, and she knew exactly how he'd be if he took her. His chest and stomach were tight with the labor, a vision to record and replay on any number of the lonely nights awaiting her back in the States.

"You feel amazing," he whispered.

Leigh replied with a scrape of her nails up his back. It riled him, as she'd hoped, and he grabbed her thigh, holding her tight as his hips sped up. The details blurred, Leigh only aware now of his hard, masculine body, his smell and his need…his strength, above all else. The desire built between her legs, deep in her core, antsy and greedy and demanding. It hardened to an ache, mirrored by the tantalizing brush of her nipples against his chest. With her longing grew his sounds, grunts deepening to moans, the noises of a man coming undone. He pressed his forehead to hers.

"Will."

Another groan and a murmured, "Please."

The orgasm burst inside her, warmth and tension and relief ringing against his erection. Her nails bit his skin but he kept stroking until the sensation was too intense, her hips begging for an end to the friction.

He flipped her onto her back and knelt between her spread thighs. Her desire flooded and surged like a riptide as he wrapped her hand around him, guiding her to stroke him fast and rough. A strangled moan tumbled from his throat as he lost himself, his release warm against her hip and fist. She touched his face with her free hand as he emptied, marveling to see him so wild, feeling he was so unmistakably hers, if only in this moment.

He flopped to his back beside her with a huff. Not willing to leave the bed, Leigh tidied herself with the far corner of the sheet, then nestled against his heaving ribs.

She broke the silence once Will's breathing slowed to normal.

"What exactly is the standard gratuity for that amenity, Captain?"

She heard his near-silent laugh, barely more than an exhalation. He mussed her hair, the teasing gesture so perfect, so comforting. So Will Burgess.

"It wasn't scheduled, so I don't mind if there's an extra fee."

"Hush, Bailey."

"Is there a meal service included, or did we not go for long enough?"

With a groan he relocated, straddling her and smothering

her cheeks and jaw in kisses, a fine manifestation of annoyance, Leigh thought.

"I'll stop, I'll stop."

"Good." He collapsed back beside her, taking her hand but leaving their overheated bodies space to cool.

Before long she felt his fingers go slack with sleep, and the fever in her skin gave way to a chill. She pulled the jettisoned covers over them, spooning herself to his side.

Liquid satin and cloud-soft cotton, but no sensation so nice as Will's presence at her back. The breeze and the rush of the waves only half as relaxing as the rhythm of his breathing.

She dropped off in no time, a final thought passing across her consciousness. She'd have no trouble sleeping in this once-intimidating bed from now on. Even alone, she'd pile the pillows at her back and imagine this feeling, and no worries would keep her from her dreams.

WILL AWOKE IN HEAVEN. Sheets like a cool breeze, early morning sunshine on his naked back, and best of all, a warm, womanly body hugged to his chest. He put his face to Leigh's hair and breathed her in.

His schedule hadn't changed in seven years, and even waking in this unexpected place, he knew it was precisely six fifty-nine—same moment he woke each day, just in time to shut off his alarm clock before it began screeching. There'd be no quick fishing trip this morning, but he wouldn't miss it. What he had here in this gigantic bed was far more fun. He pulled Leigh's long hair aside and kissed her neck and shoulder, rousing her as he reached her arm.

She shifted onto her back, smiling. He squinted at her in the dawn light, loving the sleepy look on her face, with no trace of the anxiety he so often detected there.

"Your eyes are very blue," she mumbled, the last word swallowed by a yawn.

He smiled politely, though the compliment grated. "You've got your mother's eyes," was an observation he'd heard far too many times growing up. He had her eyes. Lovely. One thing she hadn't remembered to pack when she'd disappeared with the rest of her possessions, never to return.

"Yours are gray," Will said. "I don't think I've actually met anyone with gray eyes before."

She batted her lashes at him. "They were blue when I was a baby…and once a photographer used Photoshop to make them blue for a mascara ad. Which I thought was sort of insulting."

"Gray's way more exotic."

"I like to think so."

He tried to picture her in an ad, in a magazine. On-screen. All that makeup would probably just wreck the perfection he saw right here before him. "Maybe I ought to watch one of your films."

"I doubt very much they're your taste."

"Like you know my taste after five days," he teased. "Though, actually, do you kiss other men in any of those movies?"

"I do."

"Well, you're right then—not my taste at all." He pulled her close and pressed his lips to her temple. "Good morning, by the way."

"Morning."

He ran his thumb across her lower lip. "Save the real kissing until we've brushed out teeth?"

She nodded.

"I've got to leave by nine for the morning flight. Mind if I grab a shower? Yours is a hundred times nicer than what I've got rigged on the beach."

"Give me a minute to freshen up and it's all yours. Though shout if anything exciting happens in the shower, anything you need me to spot for you," she added, bobbing her brows lewdly.

Will gave her butt a swat as she crawled from the covers. She shut herself in the ensuite and Will lay in the tangled sheets for an imaginative few minutes, replaying everything that had happened…and everything he wished had happened. Sliding inside her, that ultimate sensation of one body owning another. His cock roused, but he was relieved she'd asked that they hold back last night.

He was as nuts about Leigh as a man could be after so little time, but there was something about actual sex, actual penetration, that might've felt wrong. An arbitrary delineation, but given how close he'd come to accepting money to violate her privacy, he would've felt like a cad.

Goddamn, though—she knew how to tempt a weak man.

Water ran and quieted in the bathroom, and Leigh emerged, winding her bed-messy hair into a bun and snapping an elastic around it. "All yours."

As if he'd leave this bed, his front row seat, before she'd dressed. He watched her select panties and slide them up her legs, remembering that pale, smooth skin against his. Remembering the way she tasted and smelled, her heat when he'd slid his fingers inside to sample what they'd denied his cock.

Slipping a bright print dress over her shoulders, she put an end to Will's free show. She departed with a smirk, leaving him and his hard-on to their shower. Warm water was nice, but Leigh's hands were far nicer. Far nicer than he deserved, he reminded himself, forcing his mind off sex until he was showered and dried and dressed in his rumpled clothes. Sex rose to the forefront once more as he wondered when he might see Leigh next. And where. The big bathtub, perhaps. No, the hot tub—cool night air, steaming water, icy drinks.

He heard the television droning, already imagining how

he'd flip it off, pull her onto the couch and remind her they had far better ways to entertain themselves for the next hour.

But when he trotted down the steps to the sunken lounge, her posture told him those wishes weren't to be granted—not even close.

She was sitting on the coffee table, hugging her middle, her eyes glued to the TV. Will glanced in time to catch a photo fill the screen—a shot of Leigh standing by the counter for the airline that had taken her to Bridgetown from the States.

Real-life Leigh groaned.

The photo disappeared, replaced by the tabloid program's anchor. *"Well, it confirms the rumors—Leigh Bailey's gone on her honeymoon, but she forgot to pack her groom!"*

"That's not all she forgot," another anchor quipped, and a new photo went up, a grainy close-up of Leigh's ringless left hand.

Will sat beside her, heart in his throat. "Oh shit."

She shook her head miserably, though she looked more annoyed than traumatized.

"But that's not all. Word is, Bailey's been getting wild with the locals."

She sat bolt upright.

"No photos yet to corroborate the gossip, but a little tropical bird tells us she spent the second night of her honeymoon dancing on the sand at her exclusive island resort. And with the staff, no less!"

Leigh swore, a pair of words Will hadn't guessed her capable of. He felt cold as ice, guilt heavy, crushing his chest. It hadn't been him who'd leaked the news, but he'd come awfully close. Far too close for comfort. And he'd been the one who'd let her tag along.

"Alcohol-fueled midnight beach parties," the second anchor said. *"Doesn't sound like she's regretting her disappearing act."*

"I had one beer and it was nine at night," Leigh mumbled irritably.

"No way. And it's been 'no comment' across the board from Dan Cosenza's side." Another photo—Leigh dressed to the nines, arm-in-arm with a stylish young man in a smart suit. She snatched up the remote and shut off the TV. She tossed the clicker at the couch cushions and sat back down, rubbing her face.

"Yikes," Will offered.

She took deep breaths before she met his eyes, her gray ones glossy with tears. "Yeah, yikes. But I shouldn't be surprised."

He held his tongue.

Leigh sighed again, a weary noise. "The pictures from the airport could have been anybody, but the party… It must be one of the staff."

Invisible hands seized Will's guts, anger welling up and driving away the guilt for a moment. "Yeah, it must." Who, though, and why? This had never happened before. Who here needed easy money badly enough to compromise their job? Who needed this even worse than *Will* had? Could have been anyone. Half the staff had been at that party, and the other half would've heard soon enough through the gossip mill.

"I was stupid to think this wouldn't happen." She dropped her forehead to her hands, the picture of despair. Feeling like a shit for doing it, Will rubbed her back, trying to be supportive, though the notion felt woefully hypocritical.

"Are you going to report it?" he asked.

"No. It was my own fault, crashing that party. None of the staff deserve to get in trouble for my mistake. If anything else gets out, I will, but in the grand scheme of things, this is pretty innocuous. I'm just frustrated," she said, sounding calmer. "And disappointed. And dumb."

"You're not dumb."

"Naive, then. I walked right into that, practically invited it. Frigging Hollywood. Even on a tiny key in the middle of the ocean, you're still never free of those bloodsuckers."

"What will you do?"

"I figured I'd lie low this whole trip and clear my head, but with that all over the TV, my mom's going to have a stroke. I have to call her and try to explain."

Will couldn't help but picture that final photo, Leigh and her handsome ex. "What about your fiancé? Are you going to explain things to him?"

She shook her head. "I'm still too angry to even pretend I can be courteous to him."

"Angry?"

She nodded. "There was some…dishonesty. Right before the wedding."

"Ah."

"I don't owe him a thing. And I don't want to talk to him until I can manage it without bursting into tears. Running off was drama enough. And if he's upset that I'm having a great trip after I ran out and embarrassed him, he's got a hell of a nerve."

As a younger man, Will probably would've been relieved for the heat to be firmly directed at her ex, but he didn't just now. He felt worse, sitting here beside her, knowing he'd come so close to being the cause of her tears. No amount of money would've been payment enough, yet it so nearly had been. It drove home how deeply he felt for this woman, and so quickly. The thought unnerved him nearly as much as the guilt. He ought to steer clear. He *ought* to steer clear, but would he? *Could* he, after what they'd shared last night? She'd promised him simplicity, no expectations, but Will's heart and conscience felt tangled.

"I better head home to change," he said, standing.

She stood, too, unmistakably calmer, though her cheeks and nose were bright pink. "No coffee?"

"I better not. You've got phone calls to contemplate."

She nodded grimly. "Thank you, anyhow. For last night. For keeping me company."

"You, too."

She laughed, her heart clearly not in it. "Sorry about the drama. I swear I came here hoping to avoid all this, but…"

"It follows you?"

"It's in the job description, sadly. If I can't manage to hide here, I guess I'm just doomed. I um…" She bit her lip, staring out the window.

"Yeah?"

"Would you like to…you know. Hang out again some night?"

No way to win—say yes and feel like more of a selfish shit than ever, or say no and hurt her feelings. His hesitation seemed answer enough to deflate her.

"Sorry," she said. "That was probably inappropriate."

If she only knew what inappropriate really was, and how close he'd come to it. But stronger than his unease was his attraction, and as intimidating as it felt, his *affection* for her. It scared him to think it, but he felt…attached. But that couldn't be. Will Burgess didn't do attachment. Must be a crossed wire, his lust-clouded brain confusing guilt or protectiveness for something far deeper.

"I'd like to hang out," he admitted. "Maybe just slow things down."

"Was it weird, seeing a picture of my ex?"

That's part of it. "It was weird. Plus you could probably use some simplicity right now."

"I could. Thanks."

"Anyhow, you know where to find me."

Finally, a smile. "That I do." She stepped close and he gave her a hug, one that took a great effort to break.

"I'll let you tackle those phone calls."

She walked him to the patio door and Will slipped into his sandals.

"Thanks again," she said.

Will managed to say, "You're welcome." The second the words left his lips, his stomach dropped. Those tears drying on her cheeks could so easily have been his doing.

Only one thing for it. If he couldn't undo the mystery informant's damage, he'd just have to figure out who it was and make sure it never happened again.

The trouble was, it could be damn near anybody.

8

ONCE WILL DISAPPEARED down the beach, Leigh's favorite diversion was gone and dread rushed in to fill the void. She wished he'd stuck around, but it wasn't her fling's job to comfort her when things got complicated. That rather ruined the whole point of a fling, in fact.

He'd changed when he saw the footage, no doubt intimidated by the reality of her ex or the drama of her life back home. She'd barely been able to look at that shot of Dan, especially seeing herself, smiling at his side. That event had happened the previous fall. Had he already been cheating on her then?

But speculation didn't help her situation, so Leigh resigned herself to tackling some of the fallout. She filled a cappuccino mug with black coffee and fetched her phone, settling on the couch. As she woke the device for the first time in four days, she prayed there was no signal on Harrier Key. No such luck. Her message alerts exploded from forty-eight to over three hundred.

"Holy crap." She didn't dare check how many voice mails she had.

The thought of wading through all those messages was

too daunting, so she speed-dialed her mother. As it rang, she realized her error—it was barely 5:00 a.m. in L.A.

"Leigh!"

"Mom. Sorry. I forgot the time difference—"

"What is going *on?*" She sounded far more awake than Leigh.

"I'm on my honeymoon."

"I know that! Why? Why did you run off? Why haven't you been returning anyone's calls? Everyone's worried sick!"

"Even Dan?"

"Of course, Dan! Don't tell me you called me before you called him?"

Leigh wanted to blurt out the truth, tell her mother she'd been cheated on and that Dan loved someone else…but perhaps the saddest fact of this whole scandal was, she couldn't. She couldn't trust her mother not to tell her manager, Angela, or even the press. Not for profit, but because her mom saw any drama—or at least any that didn't paint Leigh as the bad guy—as a wise PR move, a chance for more exposure. Leigh might hate Dan for the foreseeable future, but she wouldn't sensationalize their private issues.

"I can't talk to Dan right now," she said simply.

"You have to, Leigh. You've got no idea how upset he is. He calls at least three times a day to see if I've heard from you." To find out how much she knew, no doubt. He had to suspect that Leigh had learned about his affair by now.

Leigh managed to steer the topic off Dan, asking if her mother had heard the stuff about the beach party. She hadn't yet, so Leigh summarized it. "So now it looks like I'm having the time of my life after I skipped town."

"Are you?"

The image of Will's naked body had Leigh questioning her answer. "No, I'm not. But it's good for me to be here, away from everything. Though everyone's going to think I ran off as a stunt, for the attention."

"Well, whose fault is that?"

"Wow, thanks for your support."

"I'm not going to sugarcoat this for you. But listen, that's nothing to be embarrassed about. It's not a crime to have a good time, as long as you're behaving yourself. You are, aren't you?"

Again, naked Will. "I had one beer, and I danced with a couple of the workers. Fully dressed, and I left by nine o'clock." And then proceeded to sexually assault a pilot, but no need to share that—mercifully, the informant didn't seem to have known about *that* doozy.

"The first night of your honeymoon and you're out dancing with strange men, Dan back in California a nervous wreck."

"The second night. And can we leave Dan out of this, please?"

"No, of course we can't!"

Leigh paced in slow laps around the lounge. "It's not even much of a story, though of course they made me sound like a party girl."

"Photos?"

"No, none from the party. Just the usual lame shots at the airport."

"Thank goodness for that."

Leigh stopped by the windows, staring off beyond the palms to the ocean. If only she could stay here forever, surrounded by simple beauty, thousands of miles from the chaos of Hollywood.

"Leigh, we've had dozens of offers for interviews."

"I'll bet."

"You ought to consider taking at least one of them, to clear all this up."

She rubbed at the knot in her chest. "I don't know."

"Think about it, honey. It's got to be better than letting the tabloids run wild, speculating."

"Maybe."

"I'll have Angela forward you the best offers. Give it some thought. And for heaven's sake, call poor Dan."

Oh yes, *poor* Dan. But it was true. She couldn't avoid it forever, and she'd probably enjoy this trip far more with that task behind her.

After she hung up with her mother, Leigh chugged her coffee. She'd take a shower and eat breakfast, and when the clocks struck nine in Los Angeles, she'd get to work, pick an interview and remind the people back home just how dull she really was, shut down the rumors before they mushroomed any further. Worst inevitability, she'd have to call Dan before her interview was announced. She didn't need him attacking her, anticipating she'd be outing him as a cheater on national TV or in print. She'd do her damnedest to be civil, though it burned to think he might walk away from this seemingly forgiven.

She didn't forgive him, not yet. She'd make that very clear, and pray he'd pay in his conscience for hurting her, if not in the press. It was a limp consolation, but she reminded herself it didn't matter what the world thought of her, whether they saw her as betrayed or victimized or used, or an out-of-control B-list drama queen.

The only thing that mattered was freedom from this circus, or the possibility of it, someday soon.

All in small, manageable steps. Shower. Dress. Call her manager. Call Dan, and find out where he stood. And the sooner she got her butt in the bathroom, the sooner she'd be a step closer to escaping this bullshit before the industry really did change her irreparably, as it had so many others. A hundred phone calls, one last interview…her final act of obedience before she shed the burden of being Hollywood's so-called good girl, once and for all.

LEIGH'S MANAGER OUGHT to be crowned the cell phone quick-draw champion of Los Angeles. By midafternoon nearly everything had fallen into place, thanks to Angela's efficiency. An interview offer had been selected and confirmed, lawyers consulted, contracts forwarded.

In three days Leigh would be appearing on one of the major networks' more respected talk shows for a live satellite interview. Angela already had Leigh's personal assistant arranging the technical details with the resort. Between now and then, all she needed to do was find an appropriate outfit and get her story straight.

Oh, and call Dan. Yes, how could she forget?

But her to-do list was finite, miraculously, and she no longer feared her phone. She glanced at it, sitting innocently on the counter next to her fourth cup of coffee.

With a deep breath, she picked it up and held the 2 button.

"Leigh." Dan sounded breathless. He sounded like a stranger somehow, after only a week's separation.

Leigh kept her own voice casual, though she knew she wouldn't be able to do it for long. "Hi, Dan."

"Oh my God, what's going on?"

"My mother hasn't talked to you?"

"She did, but she didn't have any answers. Why did you take off?"

Leigh wandered to the couch, feeling more tired than anything. "I sort of think you know why I took off. Do you want me to spell it out? She starts with an A, if I'm not mistaken."

A long silence. "Leigh. Don't jump to conclusions about anything you might have heard."

"Do you even know what I heard, Dan? Do you even know that after you ended your conversation with me that morning, I was still connected when you thought you'd switched back to the other line? Which, incidentally, was not a call with your brother."

More silence.

"I don't need any details. I don't want any. I know you're in love with somebody else, and I don't know if you were marrying me for the exposure or the money or what, but I don't care. It's over. Go be with her. But we need to talk about the press."

"I haven't told them anything."

Any chance of an apology? "That's good. I don't plan on telling them anything about it, either. I want this to blow over, as quick as possible. I'm going on the *Jen Landis Show* in three days to explain my runaway bride act."

"Okay."

"I don't know exactly what Angela's going to suggest I say, but nobody knows why I really ditched you. Only you and I know that." *Plus a pilot I slept with last night.* "I'm probably going to say we've been having problems for a few months, and I realized that morning that I couldn't do it. Not a meltdown, not some horrible secret. Not even a lie. Since we *were* having problems."

"Okay."

"Is that the only word you're capable of?"

"I'm sorry, Leigh."

Ah, there it was—the sting in her eyes.

"I'm sorry about what I did, and the way you found out. I never meant for it to happen, and I thought… I thought it'd be less embarrassing for everyone to deal with it after the wedding. So something like this wouldn't happen."

So I'd spend our honeymoon still hoping that we were finally going to reconnect? That hurt far too much, so Leigh steered them to practical, manageable concerns, and they hashed out a plan. Dan could deal with the condo—keep or sell it, just get Leigh's name off the deed and send her her half of the money, get her things moved to her parents' house. As for the press, they'd tell everyone the rift had been growing for some time. She'd keep Dan's indiscretions secret and he'd tell anyone who asked that he understood her decision.

Leigh stood by the plan, as much as it burned. "You are so freaking lucky I'm not there right now. I could strangle you, this is so unfair—that people are going to think I was the asshole in all this."

"I can only say I'm sorry, Leigh."

"Keep saying it, then. Just don't make me sound like a crazy person."

"I can do that." After a pause, he added, "I *am* sorry, Leigh."

"I believe you. But that doesn't make it okay."

"Of course not."

"Anyhow. I'll probably be in touch, for one thing or another."

"Okay. I'll talk to you later."

Leigh hung up. She lay on the couch, crying and deep breathing, forcing herself to feel everything. That call had gone as well as she could have hoped. She'd been afraid that he'd deny it, tell her it was a misunderstanding, or that he'd grovel and want her back and confirm her fears that he'd only ever loved her for her fame.

What he'd told her would make it easier to forgive him. Someday.

WILL WAS NAUSEOUS all that afternoon and the following morning over the state he'd left Leigh in. He'd never cheated on anyone, never caused a breakup that was anything beyond the ordinary, the excusable.

But this.

He hadn't been the one who'd wrecked her sense of security, tattling to the press, but he could've been, so, so easily.

And he felt helpless, with no hope of figuring out who'd told the tabloid about the party. He'd even called his erstwhile contact at the paper and demanded a name, but of course the man refused. All Will got was a sore throat from cussing the jerk out a second time.

Will was sitting on the edge of the dock in the afternoon, waiting for any passengers who might show for the two o'clock flight to Bridgetown. A perfect, gorgeous day worthy of a postcard, but all he could see were clouds. Somewhere nearby, Leigh was hurting, and his hopes for getting the bar open and his dad down here were back to square one. The view from square one was awfully bleak.

He'd been staring off over the water, and the vibrations of footsteps on the dock snapped him to attention. His heart stopped as he spotted Leigh, but strangely, it had nothing to do with the residual guilt. All at once he could feel the sunshine on his back, smell island blossoms on the breeze. Goddamn.

She offered a wave, a small but warm smile. She'd be okay, he realized. His heart eased, making room for those perplexing, pleasurable feelings she let loose in him.

He got to his feet. "Heading to civilization?"

"Yeah, if you've got room."

"Got nothing but."

She walked with him to the plane and took the copilot seat in the cockpit. Will got them in the air and halfway to Bridgetown before either spoke.

"I'm hoping I could charter a special flight, for this evening," she said over the engine's drone. "Around seven, if that's not too late."

"That's absolutely fine. What are you up to, in town? How did it go, talking to everyone back home?"

The longest sigh he'd ever heard answered him. "Well, I made a bunch of phone calls, and decided it's probably best that I do a TV interview, to put an end to all the rumors. So I need an appropriate outfit."

"Well, you seem very calm, considering."

She shrugged. "Actress."

They fell silent, not speaking until Will helped her down from the plane in Bridgetown.

"I'll see you at seven?" she asked.

"You will, but be punctual—sun sets around eight. Jackie usually locks up at five, so don't bother with the terminal. Just come around to the plane and I'll be waiting."

"Sounds good. I'll be early, if I can. Enjoy your afternoon."

"You, too." He watched her walk down the dock, plainly on a mission.

He spent an hour cleaning and refueling *The Passport,* then dawdled, chatting with Jackie until it was clear no one was flying back with him. No sense wasting the fuel to head home, when he had to be back for Leigh's special trip at seven. He told Jackie to head out to get ready for a date, and did all the tidying and locking up around the terminal.

What to do for the next couple hours? Grab dinner at one of his usual haunts, maybe. But no. Nothing would taste good in this mood. He knew where he had to go, the only place that could screw his head on straight, get him focused on finding a new solution, and dispel the fog that these feelings for Leigh had created in his brain.

Will's destination was only fifteen minutes on foot, and it was the perfect weather for a stroll. But he stopped in his tracks when he made it to the main road, and saw Leigh emerging from a taxi, a large shopping bag draped over her arm. She waved to him as the cab drove off.

"Wow, you're *very* early," he said.

"I found exactly what I needed in the first store. I didn't really feel like being around all those people, so I figured I'd just hang out on the dock while I waited for you. But here you are."

He nodded. "No takers on the three-thirty flight."

"Should we just head back now?"

They should, but Will's heart was set on his little side trip, and he didn't reply quickly enough.

"Did you have plans?" she asked.

"Not really." He glanced down the road.

She smirked at him. "Yes, you did. Go ahead. I can wait. I told you seven, and I can entertain myself until then."

He laughed and shook his head. "You're the worst celebrity I've ever met—hopeless at being demanding."

"Yeah, I know. But I really don't mind."

"It was nothing. I was just going to walk past that property I want to buy."

"Oh. For the club?"

He nodded.

"Can I come with you?"

"No, you can't, because I'm not going. I'm taking you back to Harrier."

"I'd love to see it."

Will would more than love to see it—he *needed* to see it. It felt like the only place he could find answers for this dilemma. "Don't you want to get back, get ready for your interview? Get your head in the game?"

"That's the last thing I want, Captain."

He hesitated. His reality check would bring anything but clarity with Leigh in tow, but he couldn't go without her, not without looking rude and suspicious. If she knew how badly he needed money, would she think him capable of doing a deal with the tabloids? It made him sick to wonder, and to know that once, briefly, he *had* been capable of it.

"Please?"

He sighed. "Yeah, okay. I'll be quick. It's just under a mile from here. Can you walk that far in those sandals?"

"No problem."

"All right then." Will stowed her shopping bag inside the terminal and locked up, and they headed down the quiet road.

"You seem blue," Leigh remarked after a few minutes.

He smiled at that. She must be having as crappy a day as he was, yet she was perceptive enough—kind enough—to pick up on his gloom. "I am."

"How come?"

"Oh, just… That gig I mentioned, the one I thought would give me enough cash to buy the place we're going to."

"It fell through?"

"It did. Wasn't worth it."

"That's too bad."

No, it's really not.

"Dare I suggest you consider selling *The Passport?* Or is that on par with auctioning off a vital organ?"

"Vital *or* reproductive, and yes. I'd sooner sell most any bit of my anatomy before I let anybody get their hands on my plane."

"Figured. Well, since your gig's wrecked, you could probably make a nice chunk of change selling an interview of your own," she said glibly.

A dagger sank into Will's heart, the pain so sharp he actually winced. Terrible enough that he'd so nearly done as much. Worse still that she thought him above it.

She touched his arm. "Sorry. I was just making a joke. A bad one. I'm really sorry that your funding's looking shaky. I shouldn't have been so flip about it."

Will's throat was too tight to reply, so he nodded. Leigh rubbed a friendly hand between his shoulder blades, and he felt his heart break—a sharp snap in his chest that hurt worse than anything he could remember. How did people live with guilt like this, day in and day out? How had his mother been able to pick up and move on, lugging this feeling around with her, heavy as a corpse?

Neither he nor Leigh spoke until they reached the shabby neighborhood that was home to Will's quickly fading dream. He waved to a couple of the locals he knew. To Leigh their leisurely loitering probably seemed like the enviable pace of island culture, but Will knew better. Far too many of this area's residents were unemployed. If he ever got his dad's club under way, he'd be proud to create a dozen new jobs, and to hopefully one day draw a steady stream of tourists to this otherwise forgotten corner of the city.

He led Leigh down a couple streets to a gravel drive.

"That's it," Will said, pointing. It was an old vacation home, once luxurious, now sun-bleached and patched with plywood.

"Wow."

He managed a laugh. "I know it's not much to look at, but it's been standing since the twenties. Built to last." He took her around the side to the real selling point, the gorgeous stretch of beach. Will had taken it upon himself to clear away the worst of the trash a week ago, when the tabloid had called and made this pipe dream seem possible.

"Oh my gosh." Leigh stopped at the edge of the sand, taking in the view.

"You should see it at sunset." Twice Will had forfeited the comfort of his bed to lie out here and nurse a few beers, dream about what he'd do with this property, fantasize about his dad's face when he finally saw the realization of his wish.

Now, though…Will felt little hope. But his father had worked his ass off to give Will everything he could, and it seemed so obvious now that he couldn't ever have repaid that selflessness with a gift funded with tabloid money, taxed so steeply at someone else's expense. And not just someone—

Leigh. Not just *someone* at all, but a woman who'd managed to burrow deeper into Will's heart than any other.

He'd taken a huge gamble, opting to grant his dad's wish the hard and slow and honorable way, but he could feel good about this place once more, even if it might not be his for two years or more. Two years his father might not have...

"So tell me about it," Leigh said. "What's your vision?"

"Where to start?" Will led her close to the water and they turned to stare at the house. It hurt to fake enthusiasm, but he put on a decent show, thinking she'd suffered enough disappointment for one day. "A huge porch or patio on the back, lots of seats, room to dance and have a live band. And I want two bars—one inside, and one right on the sand."

"And food?"

He nodded. "Grill out here, as much local food as possible. Probably not a real dinner menu, but starter-type options. More emphasis on the music and drinks. If someone in the neighborhood wants to sell me on a restaurant idea in the future, I'm open to it. But I've never done anything like this before. I'd like to keep it simple to begin with."

Leigh studied the house, as though picturing everything he was. "Would you be sad, giving up being a pilot?"

"Being a pilot was all about mobility, a job that lets me live someplace just like this."

"But owning a business will ground you."

"It will. But if I can manage to get my dad down here, I'll *want* to be grounded, for as long as I've got with him. In the future, if my wanderlust comes back, I could always sell it, if it does well."

"It'll do well," Leigh said firmly. "I can see it already."

He smiled at her. "Me, too." He could see it so clearly, even as it seemed to slip further and further from his grasp.

She sat down on the ground and Will followed suit. He checked his phone's clock. "We can't dawdle too long."

"Just a few more minutes. Tell me what else you've got planned."

"Well, lots of places to lounge. I want people to linger, and feel comfortable dropping in and shooting the shit for a few hours."

"You've got great seating right here," Leigh said, sifting the sand through her fingers.

"Indeed I do. And no televisions. No Wi-Fi. I want people to come and meet strangers and hit it off. Could be great for the neighborhood. I'll need vendors and workers, plus a few people could make a killing driving tourists back to their hotels at last call."

"The area did seem a bit rough when we were walking through."

"A cruise line used to have a port just up the beach, until the year I moved here. Then they switched to one closer to downtown, and all the tourist traffic went away. I'd love to bring just a little of it back, and see this place the way it used to be."

The conversation trailed off, and other thoughts tugged at Will. "I know you weren't eager to talk about it earlier, but how are things? Back home?"

Leigh drew the sand into a pile before her, addressing it. "Complicated. But not as complicated as it felt when that gossip broke. It was good to bite the bullet and talk to my mom. And getting a plan in place with this interview, feeling like I'm in some control of the mess I left behind."

"Good."

"But I *will* have to talk about the party during my interview, I'm afraid. I won't get anyone in any trouble, if I can help it, though. I'll be honest about basically forcing you to let me come along. And I won't mention you specifically. I'll tell them I party-crashed, since I pretty much did."

"I can't tell you how much everyone would appreciate that.

It's not a firing offense—the staff know that letting the guests have their way trumps all other policies. But it sounds like you're feeling better? About things back home?" Soon she might be missing her real life. And he'd miss *her,* he realized. What a strange sensation. Strange and vulnerable, a reminder of why he'd always endeavored to keep people at arm's length, even those he occasionally welcomed into his bed.

Leigh flattened the sand pile and traced grooves in it with her fingertips. "I'm glad I finally picked up my phone and got that out of the way, talking to my mom…and my ex."

"Oh." Will conjured up that photo again.

"It went surprisingly well."

His middle gurgled. "Well as in there's hope for the future for you two, or…?"

Leigh laughed. "Weren't you in that huge bed with me last night? Or in the shower or on the sand? Did I seem like I was praying for a reconciliation?"

Pride and relief relaxed Will's body. "No, I guess you do seem pretty over him."

"He's over me, as well." She paused before adding, "He's already moved on, actually. He moved on months ago, as far as I can tell. With someone else."

Will blinked at her, a different ache taking up residence in his chest. She'd hinted at as much before, but to know for sure…

She stabbed holes in the sand. "Please don't tell anyone I said that. I haven't even told my mom. I'm not sure why I just told you, actually."

"I won't tell a soul…. That's why you ran?"

She nodded. "I found out the morning of the wedding."

"Oh, Leigh." He stared at the sky, trying to imagine how awful that must have felt. "He told you? Or someone else did?"

"No, it was a total fluke, the way I found out. But I get now that it's been for the best, even with all this drama. I wish I'd found out well before the date so it would've just been a broken engagement, not a big, juicy scandal. But this has been a good kick in the butt for me. It just confirms that this isn't the life I want anymore. Maybe I never did."

"So what will you do instead? Any clue?"

"No clue. But I want to get far away from that nonsense, both professionally and geographically."

"Whereabouts?"

"Ooh, I dunno. Maybe someplace like this." She stretched her legs out before her, and Will tried to ignore how smooth her bare skin looked, and the memories of how it had felt against his.

He checked his phone again. "We ought to head back to the dock." He was about to stand when Leigh suddenly grasped his wrist.

"How would you…" She stared at the sea.

"How would I what?"

"This may be nuts, but maybe it's not…. Since your funding fell through," she said slowly, turning to face him, "how would you feel about letting me back you? To start your business?"

"What?"

"You need the money, and I need a project. Well, not a project—I don't want to take over your vision or anything. But something to feel invested in. A part of."

He was confused in a way he'd never experienced before, a panicky, hopeful, sickening sensation. "I'm not sure."

"I know you probably wouldn't be in a position to buy me out for quite a while, but I'd love to be a part of it. If you could get a proposal in order and all that."

Will already had the proposal—he'd pitched it to a dozen banks and been turned down for a dozen loans. He had no savings since his father's hospitalization, and his wages and the neighborhood were the reddest of red flags.

"I'm not sure," he repeated in a murmur.

"I've got a decent chunk of money in the bank, and quite a nice check coming for this interview. I'd love to help you. To fund something I actually care about, not just some anonymous stock portfolio. I know it's a bit risky, but it wouldn't destroy me if it didn't pan out. Though of course it would be a success," she added quickly.

"You're sweet to say that, but you're right, it's risky." Will had no doubt it'd succeed, though—he'd see to that personally. He turned to stare at Leigh.

"What?"

"You'd really, actually want to do that?"

She smiled. "I would. I'd be honored. And I promise I don't plan to move down here and hover around the place and micromanage every little detail. Just the money. And maybe a free drink here and there," she added with a smile.

He imagined the opposite. Leigh indeed moving down here, being a regular—perhaps even a *daily*—fixture in his life. A pleasant thought, if viewed through the lens of romantic idealism. And a strong and blinding lens it was.

"I'm still not sure. Please don't think I'm trying to patronize you, but you're at a weird point in your life. If everything's about to change for you, it's probably not the smartest time to make a huge financial commitment. I know what this island does to people, too."

She nodded. "It makes you want to feel a part of all this. But my offer…I do mean it. And obviously we're not signing papers tonight. I've got plenty of time to change my mind. And plenty of time to convince you what a genius idea it is," she added, nudging his shoulder with hers.

"You're better at coercing a weak man than you probably realize."

She gave him a beseeching look.

"I'll think about it. Now we really need to get you back to Harrier."

WILL STOLE A GLANCE at Leigh as he drove them along the gravel road to her villa, toward the setting sun. She was smiling. A small, tired smile, but a smile nonetheless. The tabloid business hadn't broken her, thank goodness.

He looked back at the road, turning her offer around in his head for the thousandth time that hour. It was the worst kind of temptation, to accept money from the woman he'd come so close to hurting. But she wanted it, badly, and his agreement could make her happy. Or was that just the rationalization of a desperate, selfish man? She had him so mixed up, he honestly couldn't be sure.

Will pulled around her drive and parked. She bit her lip as she undid her seat belt.

"What?"

"Would you like to come in?" she asked.

Will's dick wanted that, for purely selfish reasons, and his heart wanted it as well, for the mere pleasure of being near her, clothes on or off. He met her gaze. "I meant what I said this morning, about you probably needing things to be simple right now."

"I know, and thank you. I wasn't offering to throw myself at you again. But would you like a beer? Maybe you could tell me more about the club, over dinner."

He sighed, his resistance waning alongside his guilt. "Yeah, I would like that."

She opened the door and climbed out. "There are prying eyes on this island. Better not tempt fate by leaving evidence of our lurid affair parked in plain sight."

As he drove away, Will felt alive again. He felt infinitely better than he had that morning, the last time he'd said goodbye to her at her door. He could imagine what his old man might have to say about the situation. *Don't waste your time beating yourself up over the mistakes you* nearly *made. Save that for when you screw up royally.*

And Will had no intention of screwing things up with Leigh. He'd found something special with her, and though it likely would only last another week, he wouldn't waste it. He wouldn't let the chance to know her pass, and wind up regretting it once she'd flown home. All these years he'd spent determined to live without regrets.... Now wasn't the time to start overthinking everything.

He dropped his truck off and struck out on foot. The deal she'd offered wasn't something he could hang his hopes on, but it was enough to remind him that there was always another way. Enough to let him believe he'd done the right thing in telling that tabloid asshole where to stick his dirty money, and that maybe this new opportunity was the universe rewarding his decision. By the time her villa came into view, Will felt hopeful. He felt other things, as well, a fluttering in his chest, a quickening in his pulse.

Something in him was intrigued by the idea of them becoming business partners. The potential complications didn't scare him—Will tended to attract rather passionate women, and he'd navigated his share of melodramatic breakups. The only thing that did scare him was to agree to her offer, then greet her in Bridgetown a year from now only to find she had a new guy in tow. Still, he'd never been a jealous man.

Okay, that was a lie—Will had gone insane with jealousy at thirteen when he found out his mother had remarried and had another son with her new husband. That had hurt as badly as being walked out on. But he'd never feel so awful again in his life—aside from the night his father had been shot. Certainly not over a woman. Love could never be counted on to live up to its hype.

Though it was nice while it lasted.

Will bounded up the steps to Leigh's patio, noticing her hot tub was steaming. His good feelings shifted in a southerly direction. He knocked at her back door, spotting her impeccably remade bed through the glass. That would need fixing.

Leigh appeared with a glass of white wine already in hand, and slid the door aside for him.

"Why, good evening, Captain. What a pleasant surprise."

He smiled, inviting the flirtation. "Saw you have your hot tub all fired up. Now this." He pointed to her glass and closed the door behind him. "Am I interrupting your evening?"

"Even if you were, you're welcome to crash my party. I owe you one. Can I get you a beer?"

"Wine's fine," he said, following her into the kitchen. "Think I ought to prepare for a toast, if you really are serious about backing my venture."

"I'm very serious. And I'll still be very serious tomorrow and next week and a month from now. But I promise I won't rush the paperwork, so you'll know I'm not making the offer impulsively."

"You've made me other impulsive offers," Will teased.

Leigh rolled her eyes as she poured him a measure of white.

"Thanks. When's your interview? Tomorrow?"

"Day after. Tomorrow I'll be shackled to the phone, finalizing what to say, and rehearsing it endlessly with my manager, making sure the satellite link works." She beckoned for him to join her at the kitchen's shiny marble bar.

"They sending anyone out to help you? PR people?"

"No, I asked them not to. They'll be hovering plenty via the phone. It's, um… I'm very easy to coerce, unfortunately. The more persuasive people I have around me, the more I lose track of myself and what I want. I just want to be myself during the interview. Not some groomed version of me. But I do need *some* plan, so I don't get lured off topic by the host."

"Right." Will studied the condensation on his cold glass.

"Are you worried? About what I might say about the party?"

"No, not at all." The worry he did feel right now was a pleasant one, utterly tied up in how much he cared for this woman. "I'm sure you'll do fine. I hope it's the first step on the way to getting your life into the shape you want it to be."

She laughed. "Thank you. I'd actually love for it to not have any shape at all for a while, I've been corralled for so long. Would you like to toast?"

"I would." Will sat up straight and raised his glass. "To whatever will come."

"Whatever will come."

They clinked and he tasted the wine for the first time. Refreshing. Clear and clean. The way his conscience was finally beginning to feel.

"So, the hot tub," he said, raising an eyebrow at her.

"No need to sound so lurid. Friends can share a glass of wine in a hot tub," she countered, way too innocently.

"What about business partners?"

"Even more so. So can pilots and passengers."

"What about the two people who were in your bed last night?"

Finally, he got a blush out of her. "Those two are tricky. I suppose that remains to be seen."

"Shall we find out?"

"I suspect we shall."

When they reached her bedroom, she said, "Go ahead. I need to change into a bathing suit."

"Make sure it's one with a built-in chastity belt. We'll need all the help we can get, keeping this professional."

He left her and stepped out onto the patio. Cold drink, cool air, steaming water. "God bless you, Barbados."

Will stripped to his underwear and sat at the edge of the whirlpool, dipping his feet into the water. Once they adjusted, he let his calves sink into the current, then slid onto the contoured bench, churning heat engulfing him to his chest. The hiss of the sliding door announced Leigh's arrival. He turned to watch her, his scrutiny of her body in its bikini far from subtle.

"Yes?" she asked, dipping a toe in the water. "Oh my, that's hot."

"You look very nice. Don't see a lock on that suit, though."

"No, I was afraid it might rust. We'll just have to take our chances."

Will wanted to take far more than that. He smiled at the round O of her mouth as she dipped a foot into the heat.

"Too hot?"

"I'll get there." There was a rubber band on her wrist and she paused to wind her long hair into a sloppy bun. The only sexier look Will could imagine was to see it spread out across her pillow. Or his pillow. The carpet, the sand, swaying in the ocean waves. Anywhere.

"You ought to be used to this, what with your Hollywood lifestyle," he said. "Doesn't your manservant prepare your hot tub every evening?"

She smiled, sinking in the water to her hips. "I don't have a hot tub or any servants, thank you. I'm not Elizabeth Taylor, you know."

"What do you fill your Beverly Hills mansion with, then?"

Leigh laughed. "I hate to disillusion you, but my soon-to-be-former mansion is a condo. Though it does have a big whirlpool bath." She winced as she took a seat across from him, on a lower bench that immersed her right up to her shoulders and hid Will's view of her breasts. After a minute of painful faces, she draped her arms along the rim and sighed. "Okay, I've melted."

The steam lent an alluring sheen to her complexion, and with her eyes closed and her skin flushed, she looked sexy in a way Will didn't think he'd ever seen. There were so many facets to this woman, so unlike the entertainment industry visitors he'd grown accustomed to. Her desire to get out of that chaos really was genuine.

"Are you excited?" she asked, eyes still shut. Behind her, the sun sat at the horizon, edging her in a warm glow, as though she'd been dipped in gold. "Excited about the club getting off the ground? Or are you the type to withhold your excitement until things are official?"

"No, I'm not especially cautious. My dad says I've always been a dreamer."

"I could see that."

"Turn around, Leigh."

She opened her eyes and looked over her shoulder at the sunset. "Oh, wow."

"Wow, indeed."

"Why on earth would anyone *not* live here?"

Again he imagined her on the mainland, at the club so perfectly constructed in his mind's eye. Laughing and drinking and dancing on the beach. Their beach. With her neck still craned like that, he saw her pursed lips in profile. She glanced back at him.

"You want the good view, don't you?" Will slid over a few feet, making room on his side. Leigh stood and sloshed across to sit next to him. She was close…though just now, she could never be close enough, not unless they were mouth to mouth, chest to chest, legs tangled. Not until he was actually inside her.

As they watched the sun sinking, Will's body roused. The sky went from shell-pink to blazing red, to orange, to sea-green and finally indigo, without a single word spoken between them. When the first star winked to life above the ocean, Leigh's knee glanced his. Just that tiny contact struck like lightning.

They turned to face one another. Leigh's parted lips, swollen from the heat, were the sexiest thing Will had ever seen. All that separated them were six inches of hazy air—no more guilt, no more regrets.

9

SHE STARED AT WILL's handsome face, feeling scalded by his gaze. Hotter than the water... And for the first time in months, Leigh was hopeful. She beamed up a prayer that he'd let her invest in his club. This man was everything she wished she was herself, his life and his dream a compelling hybrid of wayward and dutiful. Helping him might uncover her own ambitions and dreams...or perhaps the mere helping was a worthy enough cause. In either case, she wanted to be a part of it so badly, it felt as if the longing would burst through her ribs.

And she wanted other things just as much.

She took his jaw in her hands and kissed him. His lips tasted of wine; his skin was warm against her palms. He let her lead, and Leigh didn't waste the opportunity. She kissed him deeper, her mind filling with carnal questions. Then he took over, the strong hands on her shoulder and neck making her body hum. His tongue slid against hers, hot and hungry, and she wondered how he would feel, giving her what she'd ached for when he'd knelt before her in the shower.

Her breath caught as his hand slid to her breast. His touch had been eager both times they'd fooled around, but he felt different tonight—possessive, with no trace of hesitation.

As he palmed her inside the cup of her bikini top, their kissing became a distracted press of lips, light grazes and shared breath. He made her feel all those things she'd missed out on. Breathless first love—the real-life kind, with no script dictating the experience.

She ran her hand down his chest into the hot water, before taking the caress lower. He was hard behind the cotton of his shorts, just as she'd known he would be. His touch tonight was self-assured and fearless, and she couldn't wait another minute to discover how that would translate to the rest of his body's demands. She pulled away.

"Let's go inside."

Will smiled. "As you wish."

She straightened her top, switched off the tub and climbed out, skin tensing in the cool air. An electrifying sensation, like Will's proximity. She padded to the entrance. His wet hand alighted on her side as she slid the door open, chills turning to heat in an instant.

He nearly shut the door before seeming to recall her request from the night before. He opened it again, inviting in the smell and sounds of the ocean.

"So. We've defiled your beach, your shower, your hot tub, your bed…. Anywhere else you want to have your way with me?"

She put a finger to her chin, pretending to consider. "We've covered all my bases. What about your truck? Cabin of the plane?"

He stepped close, smiling.

"Your hammock?" she suggested. "Or whatever it is you sleep in."

He kissed her and Leigh lost the will to banter. They both knew it was bed or bust. She let the idea percolate a moment… *honeymoon suite.* Sans husband, which only made it more forbidden and thrilling. She pulled back again, grinning at him.

"What?"

"Hang on." She returned to the patio, fetching their glasses. Carrying them inside, she passed Will and headed for the kitchen. "Follow me."

She poured out their chardonnay and opened the fridge, sliding the bottle of champagne from its special slot in the door.

He watched as she unwound the metal cage from the cork, then he put his hand out. "That's a man's job."

Leigh passed it over.

"Before I open this, what are we toasting?"

"My honeymoon." For a second she wished she could take it back, wanting to give Will no reason to think he wasn't the only man on her mind. But he merely grinned.

"Your honeymoon?"

"Yes. To it going far better than expected."

His gaze darted to the open bedroom door, and she knew he was imagining the same guilty pleasures she was. "If you're willing to pretend to play the part of my husband, that is." Why did the idea fill her chest with such a floating, weightless sensation? The wine's fault, surely.

Will twisted the cork until it popped, vapor rising from the bottle. "At the rate I'm going, this may be the only honeymoon I get."

"Don't be stingy," Leigh directed as he poured. They clinked their glasses and drank, the fizz of the wine just right, matching the excitement bubbling through her body.

They kissed between sips, and Leigh decided this was how champagne ought to be enjoyed—off the lips of one's clandestine lover.

When they set their empty glasses aside, she offered Will a mischievous look and started toward the bedroom.

"Wait, wait, wait." He jogged to catch up. "You're skipping the most important bit." He caught her behind the knees, hauling her up into his arms.

"Oh yes, the threshold. You're awfully good at this. You're sure you haven't been a groom before?"

"Quite sure. But it never hurts to practice." He carried her through the door and dumped her unceremoniously across the bed.

"Not the smoothest landing," Leigh teased, sitting up.

"Emergency situation. Very urgent. Do we have any...?"

"Bathroom, top drawer."

Will returned with a fistful of foil-wrapped condoms.

"Ambitious," Leigh said.

He merely smiled, setting them on the nightstand. He looked around the room for a moment, spotting the shelf above the other bedside table, arranged with candles. He got the pillars lit and switched off the lights.

"You don't have to seduce me," she teased. "I'll go without a fight."

"On the contrary. This is your honeymoon, Miss Bailey. Or are you Mrs. Burgess now?"

"No, you're Mr. Bailey. We're a very progressive couple."

"That's Captain Bailey to you, Mrs. Burgess."

Crawling over the bedspread, Will covered her body with his. Everything felt right—the heat coming off his bare chest, her wet swimsuit against the dry linens. He planted his knees between hers and nudged them wide, dropping to his elbows, their faces so close their noses touched.

Leigh wished she knew the perfect thing to say...something intimate, something like "I love you," but for casual lovers. She settled for, "This is very nice."

He kissed her chin. "Yes, it is."

"I...I'm very fond of you."

He pulled back enough to let her see his broad smile. "Are you? You must be terribly drunk. I like that in a woman."

She swatted his arm.

"I'm very fond of you, too," he said, then lowered to swipe his lips against hers.

Satisfied on the sweet-nothings front, Leigh let more carnal needs assert themselves. She ran her hands down his back, relishing the feel of his shoulders, the twin ridges of muscle flanking his spine, the firm shapes of his hips and backside. He brought their bodies closer, close enough for his erection to brush her mound and set her pulse pounding.

"Will."

He kissed her, deep, sensual sweeps of his tongue that matched the stroke of his cock. As she wrapped her legs around his waist, his moan warmed her lips. He angled his hips, his hard length taunting her through their damp layers. She slid her hands under his waistband to memorize the motions as he thrust, and imagine how he'd feel when he was actually making love to her. No, no—having sex with her, she corrected. Very, very fond sex.

"What do you want?" he whispered.

"Just you."

"That's encouraging. But we're not in any hurry...."

"What about you? You can have just about anything you want, Will."

He pushed up, bracing his arms by her sides. "What I want is to wreck you for every other man you'll ever meet. Any tips on how to go about that?"

She laughed. "You're a pilot living in a tropical paradise. You're quite tough to top as it is."

"What's your favorite thing? In bed?"

She frowned thoughtfully. Having Will here, excited and exciting, was the greatest turn-on she'd ever experienced. "I'm not especially adventurous, to be honest. I just like feeling all...crazy, with you. And making you pant. That's very sexy. Tell me how I can drive you insane."

"The fact that we're not naked yet is a good start. But if you mean the good kind of insane, I say we lose the clothes and roll around. And when it looks like you've made me wait so long I might have a heart attack, then you'll have reached your goal."

Liking this idea, Leigh arched her back and angled her arm to get her top untied. Will lifted it away and tossed it to the floor. For a long minute he spoiled her with caresses, thrilled her with his hungry gaze. When he finally bent down to take her in his mouth, her need went from romantic to aggressive in an instant. She held his head and stroked his hair, admiring his face, so placid with his eyes closed. She tried to imagine another expression, the one he'd wear when he took her, and the seconds before his pleasure came to a peak. All those noises she'd heard when she'd been before him on her knees in the sand. The memory of how he'd tasted from the ocean had her mouth watering.

Will slid farther down the bed, trailing kisses from her ribs to her navel, her hip bone, the outside of her thigh. His touch felt at once familiar and new as he dragged her bottoms down her legs. Settling on his forearms between her knees, he slipped one hand beneath her butt, the other grazing the crease of her innermost thigh. He brought his mouth mere millimeters from her sex, so close she felt his warm breath when he spoke.

"I've been imagining this for ages."

"Since two nights ago, you mean."

She could just make out his smile. "Feels like an eternity."

Any reply she had evaporated when his lip touched her clit. She fisted his hair, earning a noise of distinct, happy approval.

Leigh shut her eyes, filled her head with fantasies. As Will's tongue traced the seam of her sex, she conjured the vision of his naked body, of soapy water sliding down his chest and stomach. She'd dated few men, all of them sexy in their own ways, but none like Will. He had no constructed style, no self-conscious image, and he only seemed more like himself with his clothes off. She'd never gotten so hot, merely picturing a man's bare body before.

As his tongue teased her clit with firm, slick sweeps, she imagined him above her, penetrating her. She'd gotten a taunting taste the night before of how he might be—frantic yet masterful—and she hoped it was an accurate preview. Remembering what he'd said, she felt a flush of pride to believe he'd never done this before, been in one of the villa's extravagant beds.

Will kept his tongue teasing, and the hand that had been idly kneading her thigh inched closer, closer, until she felt his fingertips at her entrance. She heard him suck in a breath, evidence of his surprise or excitement when he found her wet for him. Her body gave no resistance as he slid two fingers inside, then a third. He eased them deep, then drew them out, over and over, and she replaced them with his cock in her mind's eye.

"I want you," she murmured.

This time when he spoke, his breath felt cool against her overheated clit. "I want you, too."

She smiled to herself. "It was supposed to be me who was driving *you* crazy right now."

He laughed. "You don't think you are?"

"Prove it."

Will spoiled her rotten with his mouth for another minute, then rose to his knees between her legs. The bulge in his shorts looked hard and heavy. He smiled at her and ran his hand along his ridge. "This enough proof for you?"

"More than enough." More than enough waiting, as well.

Will seemed to agree. He got out of bed, easing his shorts over his erection and kicking them away. His body was gorgeous in the warm light, strong and sexy and perfect.

He knelt before her, and for a dangerous moment, she imagined this *was* her honeymoon, this man really her husband. He would never bore her, never steer them into a life governed by bills and obligations and the other hallmarks of a typical, mundane existence. He'd keep her on her toes, fly her wherever she wished to explore. He'd take her to bed in some remarkable little home on the mainland, a tropical breeze pushing the curtains in. Swimming, laughing, being lazy, making love.

Love. A scary, wonderful word she didn't dare assign to a man she barely knew. No, this was infatuation—the hottest of new loves, more thrilling than a mere crush, more primal and urgent than the slow transformation of friends to lovers.

Will's face had changed in a most alluring way…that heaviness in his lids, that parting of his lips.

"Are you crazy yet?" she asked.

"Certifiably."

She reached to the bedside table and handed him a condom, keeping her eyes on his ready cock as he wrestled the rubber from its fancy foil packaging. Even the way he sheathed himself was a perfect seduction, three seconds that felt like an hour's torturous wait. As he lowered his body to hers, time stood still. Every tiny detail—the dip of the mattress, the smell of his skin and the lubricant of the condom, the heat of his breath—coalesced to make this the most erotic moment of her life.

"Ready?" His tone was soft and sincere, with no teasing for a change.

She nodded. "I'm ready."

"You're *nearly* ready," Will corrected. He turned her head on the pillow and tugged the elastic from her bun, then mussed her hair. "There. Perfect."

Leigh ran her hands down his body, paying extra close attention to the firm crests of his abdomen and the groove of his hips. She swept the backs of her fingers along the under-side of his cock and Will groaned. He reached between them to fist his shaft, guiding himself to her lips.

"Will."

He eased the first two inches inside.

Longing turned to lust in a flash, and she drew her short nails up his back. His hips bucked, giving her half his length as he swore.

"More," she whispered.

He drew himself out, the second taste of penetration as hot as the first. This time he gave her more, enough for her to be sure she'd never been with a man this big before.

"Feels amazing," he murmured, his attention fixed be-tween their bodies.

She tugged at his sides. "More."

He withdrew and took her to the same depth again, again. Finally, when her nails bordered on clawing, he sank deep, until they met utterly, belly to belly, hip to hip. She shut her eyes and steeped herself in the moment, memorizing the tiny pulsations beating between them.

Without warning, he turned them onto their sides, hold-ing her top leg tight to his waist. His thrusts started small and slow, with kisses to match. As the kissing deepened, his cock grew insistent, his strokes turning long and explicit.

She freed her mouth to take a breath. "God, Will."

"Leigh." He pulled away to steal a glance between their bodies, looking as disbelieving as she was that this could feel as right as it did.

With his rhythm steady, she joined in, complementing his thrusts with the movements of her hips. Her body's demands excited him, and she gasped when he turned them again, her on top. She sat upright, and had to smile at the view—of this strong and shameless man looking so helpless beneath her.

She settled herself atop him, finding the right place for

her knees so she could slide all the way off, then take every inch back inside. She listened to his moans and sighs, and watched him watching her.

"Give me your hands," she said, beckoning.

Will raised his arms, letting her interlace their fingers and use his hands for balance as she rode him. She took his cock at a sharp angle, the friction of his shaft against her clit transforming her from excited to wild.

"God, Leigh." His words were followed by a groan, his strained expression proof that he wanted this as badly as she did. As something beyond mere sex. Something powerful and pure.

Their palms grew slick. As she neared release her strokes turned frantic.

Will's gaze was pained, but his voice strong. "Please."

She let herself go, concentrating on how good he felt inside her, how right. The pleasure became a harsh streak, heating her sex and belly and chest, flashing bright each time her clit stroked his cock. She felt him suppressing thrusts of his own, hips shifting beneath her. Her breath grew shallow as the sensations pooled between her thighs, hot and demanding.

"Don't stop."

No chance. She rode him fast as the pleasure mounted, until the sensation and the need to release was greater than she'd ever felt before. "Will."

"Please."

The climax pulled her under and turned her inside-out, seconds of exquisite bliss that felt they went on far longer. Better even than the pleasure was the sound of Will losing control beneath her. As she came down from the rush, she felt his fingers between hers, heard his labored breaths.

"Did you…?" she asked.

"Not yet."

"On top," she murmured.

Will nodded and let her hands go, and Leigh flopped onto her back. As he knelt between her thighs, he seemed rattled—clumsy, impatient, needy. That she'd brought him to this state filled Leigh to the brim with pride. He guided his cock to her, taking her slowly, as deep as they could go.

"Will…"

This was exactly how she wanted it to be, when he gave in. The perfect view of his body, taking what it needed from hers. She stroked his arms as he found his pace, quick and steady, with nothing to prove.

Feeling shameless, she asked, "Can you lean back a bit?"

He complied, chest and face cast in the golden candle-light. Leigh feasted on the flex of his muscles as he took her.

"You look amazing."

He smiled, his knitted brow giving away his mania. "I'm close. I don't want it to be over yet."

"We've got plenty more nights ahead of us." She meant her vacation…didn't she?

"You're right," Will said.

He grabbed her knees, hugging her thighs to his hips and letting loose. Leigh tried to match his thrusts, but there was no way—he pounded her hard for a noisy final minute, then gave in. As he came, a groan spilled from his throat and he drove deep for one, two, three spasms. His grip went slack, and slowly, a grin took over his face.

Leigh laughed.

He eased out and got rid of the condom, then tumbled onto the covers beside her. They lay in silence for several minutes, until their racing breaths slowed to the rhythm of the waves lapping the beach. Then he turned his head and smiled at her.

"Good honeymoon?" she asked.

"Best honeymoon I've ever had."

"Me, too. So good we forgot to order any dinner."

"Food wasn't foremost on my list of needs tonight," he said.

"No, mine either. That was way more satisfying."

"You going to tip me for my exceptional room service?"

She nudged his ribs with her elbow, then sighed, far too content even to flirt. Will rolled onto his side, draping an arm over her waist and nestling his face against her neck. It was a more tender gesture than she'd come to expect of him. She stroked his hair, wanting to return the affection.

"I like you way more than I should," he said softly.

Leigh blinked up at the canopy, her chest fluttering anew. "How do you mean?"

"I like you a lot more than *anybody* should, considering how long we've known each other."

She took several deep breaths before replying. "I feel that way, too."

"You're just vacation-drunk. You'll get over that. But me… I'm a goner."

"Will that make the club proposition a bad idea?"

He shrugged. "Not for me. I'm well trained in awkward breakups. I can keep things professional after you come to your senses and dump me."

She combed her fingers through his messy hair. "We're not a couple, so nobody can dump anybody."

"True. And maybe that's the way it ought to stay."

"Maybe? Did you have something else in mind?"

Will sighed, faking weariness. "Only to trick you into falling in love with me the next time you're in the area, checking on your investment. But if you'd rather avoid the unpleasant chore of cutting me loose after you realize your error, we can keep it casual."

"Listen to you. You make it sound like I'm the one in this bed who hates feeling tied down."

"I'm shiftless," Will said, "but I'm not stupid. If I thought I had a chance with a woman like you, I'd get you drunk and order a justice of the peace from the front desk."

She laughed. "I don't know exactly why you think I'm so astounding, but I won't argue."

"No, do. I love bickering with you." He kissed her neck and held her close, his caresses growing lazier as the breaths at her ear turned deep and calm.

The promise of this affair continuing one day, with the chaos of her present firmly in the rearview mirror, had Leigh breathing easy herself. She had something that made the next few weeks' and months' worries worth tackling head-on, a destination she could chart, not merely be carried to. As Will fell asleep against her, her burden felt light, no more than an annoyance. An interview, a house sale, the placation of her parents once she announced her retirement from the Hollywood scene. Then freedom. She nearly welcomed the stress back home, knowing the next time she touched down at LAX, it might be for the last time. Goodbye to the business, hello to the future and its blessed unknowns.

It was so odd, lying here with Will. She'd been with Dan for over two years, trusting him implicitly, only to be hurt. But with Will…she'd known him a handful of days, their courtship as fast and reckless as hers and Dan's had been steady, calm. Yet she felt no fear with Will. As crazy as it was, she trusted him without question. Trusted him with her life in a plane, with her body and heart in this bed. If a crash was in the cards, she didn't want to know until the shore and sea were already rushing up to meet her.

LEIGH SMILED upon opening her eyes. A sleeping, slack-mouthed Will Burgess was a nice sight to be greeted by first thing in the morning. The sun was low and it couldn't be later than six, but she was instantly brimming with energy.

She untangled herself from Will's arm and the covers, and padded to the bathroom, then to the kitchen to get the coffee going.

He'd have to leave by nine for the morning flight, but perhaps she could persuade him to stay for breakfast...or another roll in the 600-thread-count hay. She grinned at such a thought. Sleeping with Will was proving a very effective mood stabilizer.

She sat on the couch with her coffee and the resort activities binder, and even when she stared right at the television's dark screen, she felt no desire to turn it on and scour the toxic entertainment channels. Instead she flipped through the offerings, everything now sounding as delightful as it had sounded dismal her first day. *Surfing lessons, as conditions permit.* If conditions permitted, she might just give that a shot.

"Good morning."

Leigh jumped as Will's hand alighted on her shoulder from behind. "Oh, jeez—don't sneak up on me. I'm armed." She held up her steaming mug. "And good morning."

He planted a kiss on the crown of her head. "Indeed it is."

Leigh smiled, pleased by his flirtatious tone. He'd seemed so down yesterday afternoon, but today he was a new man. She knew her offer of funding had much to do with that, and it made her proud. It made her believe that yes, this was a good decision. The right decision, and one she'd thought up all by herself.

"Do you have time to stick around for room service breakfast?" she asked.

"I had a better idea, if you're interested."

"Oh?" She moved to her knees on the couch to face him.

He smoothed her hair behind her ears, the gesture so fond and natural, she blushed with pleasure.

"It's early enough to take you out fishing, if you'd like."

"I'd love that."

He smiled, looking obscenely handsome. "Great. Let's chug some coffee and we'll head to my place."

Will fetched a mug and sank into the easy chair. Leigh

took the liberty of propping her heels on his thigh, liking the familiarity of the scene.

"You're cheerful this morning," he said, toying with her big toe.

"I could say the same about you."

"Yeah, but you must have a lot on your mind."

"Sure. But after tomorrow's interview, I'll be free. The end is in sight for me. And at the risk of sounding too eager or jumping to any conclusions, I'm really excited. You know, about the offer I made you."

His smile was slow and warm. "I'm excited, too."

Hope did a somersault in her middle. "So you're still interested? You'll definitely consider it?"

"I will indeed. It's a tough offer to pass up, especially since that other source of funding fell through."

"You ever going to tell me what that mysterious gig was?"

"Just a private contract thing. As big as the payout might have been, it wasn't worth it."

"Too much hassle?"

"Just too shady."

"Too shady for Captain Bribery? You astound me. What was it? Trafficking smuggled parrots or something?"

"Or something."

"Well, I'm glad you're intrigued by *my* offer."

He flexed her toes forward and back. "I find you very intriguing on the whole. The only trouble I can foresee is our romantic entanglement complicating our business entanglements."

"Have I entangled you?"

"Oh yes, thoroughly. On the beach and in the shower, and the tub and your bed. And I won't stop you from entangling me again this evening, if you're keen."

"Shameless."

Will grinned and drained his mug. "Let's head out."

As they walked down the beach, he did something Leigh had hoped he might—he took her hand in his.

She gave it a squeeze. "This entanglement is all you."

"We'll need to disentangle when we get close to the town, so we don't cause any more scandals."

"Have you taken much flak from the others, for bringing me to that party and making everyone complicit?"

"No. I mean, nobody's names were given in the story. And no one's going to rat anyone else out, not in this crooked little burg."

"Not even the person who spoke to the press?"

"I doubt it. I've known everyone on this island for years, and I think whoever's doing it, it's only out of desperation. I honestly don't think they'd say anything to hurt anyone. Any of us, I mean. Sadly, they were willing to hurt you." His expression darkened.

"At least it's only been the one story. Maybe they just needed easy money."

"Let's hope so."

The edge of town came into view and Leigh regretfully dropped Will's hand. He stopped walking to face her.

"Yes?"

"Thank you," he said firmly. "For the offer. And for last night."

"Thank you for considering. And for last night. *Especially* for last night."

He took a step closer. "In just a few yards we've got to go back to faking innocent acquaintance."

Leigh looked down and drew a line in the sand with her toe. "We're still on this side."

"Yes, that's true." Will glanced along the beach before he reached out and grasped her by the waist, lowering his mouth to hers.

Leigh melted. From the contact, and the openness of it,

and from the way it felt like so much more than a mere fling now. She wrapped her arms around his shoulders and deepened the kiss, loving his height and warmth as she stood on her tiptoes and pressed herself to him.

This interesting, passionate, surprisingly driven man… Better than anything she'd hoped to find on this tiny island. The present felt like clear skies, with doubt and clouds blown far away.

10

"EVERYONE, please join me in welcoming Leigh Bailey to the show!"

Leigh smiled through the applause. She needed no set; the villa's living room was already perfectly styled. The staff had added extra flowers to the table beside her and arranged the video linkup. She'd be live in the eastern and central times zones, then two hours behind, farther west. Jen Landis's beaming face stared at her from the monitor. Thankfully, this was the only angle Leigh got, so she wouldn't have to see herself or the audience during the live interview. That'd be too weird to handle. But she felt prepared. She knew her script, as it were, the healthy mix of evasiveness and honesty she and Angela had hashed out.

"Hi, Jen. Thanks so much for having me."

"Thank *you* so much for sharing your story with us."

Leigh smiled, letting her shyness show.

"To say you've had an interesting couple of weeks is an understatement. America is itching to know why you ran out on your fiancé, Dan Cosenza, the morning of your very public and very *expensive* wedding. Not to put you on the spot, but let me ask the question everyone is dying to have answered—was it a publicity stunt?"

"Definitely not. I like to think I'm pretty low-key. For an actress."

Jen laughed warmly and Leigh relaxed a little.

"As much as I've enjoyed working in front of cameras, I'm pretty cagey about the spotlight, even the red carpet. Trust me, it was never my intention to cause a stir."

"Why, then?"

Leigh bit her lip. "Forgive how ridiculous it might sound, my saying this when I've agreed to an interview…but the reasons for the change of heart are private, between Dan and myself. Like any other couple, we had our issues. I take responsibility for downplaying those issues, and winding up with enough doubts that I had to call things off the morning of my wedding."

"That can't have been easy."

"It's hard to describe, to people who aren't part of the celebrity culture." She caught herself fussing with her hair and willed her hands to behave. "There's just so much swirling around you, so much chaos. It's easy to get swept up in it and not notice the more subtle things happening in your life."

"Problems in your relationship, you mean?"

"Absolutely. The energy of the city and the job can drown everything out. And that morning, for whatever reason, I just couldn't ignore the little whispers in the back of my head any longer." She felt her first twinge, confirming her fears—she'd probably wind up crying on national television.

"But why go on your trip, Leigh? Surely it's got to be a painful reminder of your failed relationship, sleeping in the *honeymoon suite* without Dan?"

Without Dan, but certainly not alone, Leigh thought, with a flash of not entirely unpleasant guilt.

"It is, but… We don't have any memories together here. Staying home after I chose to not go through with the wedding would have been too confusing and painful. I hoped taking off would give both of us time apart to think, and for me to get myself calmed down before I came home and faced the media. I hadn't planned on doing any interviews, to be honest…and no offense to you, Jen."

"Of course not."

"But when things started getting leaked and blown out of proportion, my family got frantic from everyone inundating them with questions about me. I had to just get it all out there, officially."

"So are you and Dan speaking?"

Leigh nodded. "We are. There are hurt feelings on both sides, but we're talking."

Jen's angular eyebrow rose as high as Botox allowed. "Any chance of a reconciliation?"

Leigh laughed, more nervous than surprised. "No. We both agreed that we need things we just weren't getting from each other. The decision was mutual. And final."

Jen pouted. "You two seemed so happy."

"I know we did. And for the first year and a half, we really were. When he proposed, I was absolutely head over heels in love with him. But anyone will tell you, people change. Especially people in the spotlight." The first tears arrived and she wiped them with her wrist. "Sorry."

"Not at all." Jen smiled. "I'd hand you a tissue if I could."

"The celebrity thing is a tough storm to weather, and Dan and I just weren't strong enough to make it through as a couple. We're both still young and have a lot of growing up to do before we can make that commitment, I realize now. But I wish him the best."

"And it sounds like he wishes you the same." True. Dan had lived up to his promises to paint her kindly in the press. "Now, Leigh. Let's talk about some other things."

Leigh smiled and sighed, knowing what was coming. "Okay, Jen. Bring it on."

"You've been busy on your solo honeymoon, or so we hear."

She laughed. "Yes. That rumor about me crashing a local party is true. But I promise you, it wasn't nearly as wild as people wish it was. A bit of dancing and one drink and I was in bed by ten, former Girl Scout's honor." She made the sign with her fingers.

"But it's not all boring though, is it? Come on, Leigh. What about the new mystery man?"

Leigh blinked, her brain suddenly swallowed by static.

"Oh, we've got her," Jen teased. "It's just making the papers now, so here's your chance to get your side of the story told. What exactly is the deal with you and this William Burgess?"

"Will?" she said dumbly.

"Say whatever you like about the party rumor, but I've got to tell you, Leigh, the passion in those pictures is hard to deny. Do we have them?" The talk show host looked to the side, to some unseen production person. The camera swiveled in time for Leigh to watch a photo fill the stage's huge screen. Her belly filled with bricks. She and Will, hand in hand on the beach. Then kissing. No mistaking the lip-lock for a friendly flirtation. The shots were grainy, but she hadn't been quick enough to deny it was her. And whoever had sold the photos must also have taken it upon themselves to supply Will's identity, maybe earned themselves a nice bonus in the process.

The camera swung back to Jen's face, the audience still oohing. "Now come on, Leigh. You can't downplay that one."

"Um, no. Will and I… We've had a bit of an unexpected romance." Her heart pounded, so hard she felt a head rush coming on.

"I'll say." The camera swiveled again, allowing Leigh to see a crisp, candid shot of a shirtless Will standing beside his boat. "And I think all the ladies in the audience will agree, you do know how to pick a rebound, right?" More whooping and Jen's face returned. "But is that all this is, Leigh? A rebound?"

"I don't like that term, but yes, I suppose that's what some people might call it. It's just one of those things that happened."

"Still, it's very unorthodox, Leigh. I mean, you run off alone on your honeymoon, dodging the press, and who should you fall for but a man who was in cahoots with the tabloids to report on you?"

Leigh's body turned to stone—heavy, cold, numb.

"Is love really that crazy? Or could we maybe be honest here. You want the press attention, don't you, Leigh?"

"Pardon me?" She could barely make out Jen's words.

"The tabloids have spilled about your new man having been in bed with them. Don't you think it's your turn?"

Leigh was speechless, so Jen went on. "Admit it, why are you on with us right now? Publicity is nothing to be ashamed of. It makes Hollywood run. But let's be straight. Did you in fact have an agreement going with Will Burgess, to have him feed rumors to the press about you?"

Deer in the headlights. Leigh was silent for perhaps another five seconds, though they felt like an eternity. Will was the informant? Her breath sped with her pulse and she panicked, having no clue if she should deny it, admit her ignorance.… Damn it, where was Angela when she needed her? Back in L.A., that was where, and she could practically hear her swearing a blue streak all those thousands of miles away. "I didn't hire Will to report about me," Leigh finally mumbled.

"How did you feel when you found out, then? Did he tell you before or after your romance had begun?"

"After," she said numbly.

"That must have been a blow."

"Yes, you could say that."

"Are you all right, Leigh? This seems painful for you to talk about."

She gathered her wits. "It is, sure. But Will and I aren't... you know. We're not a couple. And I didn't know about those photos. I had nothing to do with anything being...staged. Or planned."

"Is it true your new man is a pilot?" More lurid oohing.

"Yes, he is." Wasn't he? Or was he just a reporter with a pilot's license?

"And you two never met before your so-called honeymoon for one?"

"No."

"So it was a real whirlwind romance?"

"I guess."

"Any plans for the future, or are you just going to fly right out of this pilot's life forever?"

Leigh spoke slowly to keep from stammering. "Like I said, it's just something that happened."

The rest of the interview felt like figments from a fever dream. Leigh answered questions flatly, her heart pounding so hard she feared she'd faint, live on television. Jen's voice and face were surreal sounds and shapes, Leigh's responses detached from her own mouth. It seemed to go on forever, a nightmare she couldn't wake from.

But eventually Jen said, "I'm afraid we're just about out of time. But before we let you get back to your honeymoon—" a pause for audience laughter "—what are your plans? What's next for Leigh Bailey?"

"I'm not sure yet. I'll probably take a break from acting, though. I'm keeping my options open for the time being."

"And what about William Burgess? Do those plans include him?"

"No. No, I don't think so."

WILL'S PHONE CHIMED as he was heading down the dock after tidying the plane following the day's final flight. His heart gave a leap, imagining it was Leigh, calling to share how her interview had gone. But he realized as he dug out his cell that she didn't have his number. He checked the screen and hit Talk.

"Hey, Jackie. Emergency pickup?"

"William!" Her energetic voice was more shrill than usual. "Emergency, yes. What's this I'm seein' on my TV?"

"Pardon?"

"Leigh Bailey's on one of them talk shows!"

"Yeah, it's live, from her villa. You're watching it?"

"Jus' what is this all about, you takin' money from the tabloids?"

Will's universe shrank, reduced to the texture of the aluminum planks beneath his feet. "What?"

"They just said, on the show. You been sellin' stories about her to the press. And you two been havin' an affair?"

"She said all that?"

"No, the host said all that. And they got pictures of you two! William Burgess, I am so disappointed."

"I never took any money from the press."

"Well, everybody seem to think you has."

Including Leigh? "Shit."

"Very deep shit, too. You gon' get yourself fired, and I'm gon' have to explain all this to the customers. If we *get* any more customers after this mess."

"I have to go."

"Yes, you go. You go fix what you done before we all cooked. What celebrity ever gon' fly with us again after what you did?"

"Don't panic, Jackie. I'll figure this out."

Will ended the call and stared blankly at the water for a minute or more.

What on earth had Leigh been told? Even if it was merely the truth, that he'd once agreed to report on her...that was plenty. It didn't matter that he'd changed his mind. The fear drove deep, a sharp, ragged pain. He'd be fired for sure. He could feel his father's dream tumbling away, slipping from between his fingers, disappearing into the deepest, blackest pit of hopelessness.

Worse even than that, Leigh must think he was a monster.

And was he? He'd tried as hard as a man could to take it all back.

The only woman he'd ever...hell, yeah. That he'd ever *loved*. Admitting that to himself only sharpened the sting. The only woman he'd ever loved and he'd hurt her, wrecked her belief that he really did value her for who she was. She must think he'd done everything he had with only a price tag in mind. Their friendship and flirtation, their lovemaking. And Jesus, he'd accepted her promise of funding for the club. She had to be dying inside, eaten up by hurt and betrayal, feeling foolish and used. This wasn't how karma was supposed to work.

He remembered something then. That very afternoon, heading to Bridgetown, he'd had two vacationing passengers in the cabin, plus Rex in the cockpit. His friend had been uncharacteristically edgy throughout the flight, chatting about his latest female-related drama. He'd been far more at ease and animated on the ride back, unmistakably relieved, with an envelope tucked in his shirt pocket...

Will shoved his heartache to the back of his mind and marched down the dock. He knew Rex's vehicle by the dent on the bumper, and it hadn't left the lot yet. Will broke into a sprint.

He found Rex in the driver's seat, talking on the phone with a wide smile, colorful bills in his hand. When Will thumped the glass, shaking with anger, Rex slid the money under his thigh and ended his call. He rolled down the window and slapped a huge grin on his handsome face. "Hello, again, Captain."

"It was you," Will said. "You did a deal with the tabloids."

Rex didn't bother giving him a song and dance; his smile wilted into a grimace of guilt.

Will shook his head, shocked. Could he really be so scandalized, though? He'd come awfully close to holding those bills himself, and only an unexpected loyalty to Leigh had kept him back. All he could do was demand, "Why?"

Rex slumped. "I had to, man. My sister's in a bad way up in Prospect. Her baby's sick and her man left her, and she got fired for missin' work to take the child to the hospital."

Will sighed, feeling as lost as ever. Rex's need was as legit as his own had ever been....

"I had to," Rex repeated, obviously panicked that Will was going to report him.

"You took pictures of *me* with her. Pictures that could get me fired." As if the fact that Will had spoken to the papers in the first place wasn't enough.

"They was blurry, man. Nobody could tell it was you."

"They know now."

"I di'n tell them, I swear it."

It was possible. If Will had never made himself a target, cussing out that editor, he maybe could have *stayed* an anonymous blur. He saw the regret in Rex's eyes, pained and genuine.

"I'm sorry, Will, but come on. What else I got? You own your vehicle, man." He nodded to the bobbing plane. "I got shit. A shack on the beach and a weekly check... I can't lose this job, Will. I'll split the money with you, if you keep quiet. Ten grand, they paid me. I can give you three, but the rest... I need it, Will. My sister needs it. My baby nephew."

Will glanced at *The Passport,* his life's savings, his ticket to elsewhere. He could have chosen to strand himself, sell the plane and bring his dad here. *Too high a price,* he thought. But was it? What was his precious freedom worth, when he stacked it against his father's happiness, or the honor of the woman he'd come to love so fiercely in so little time?

"Please, man." Rex was counting out bills on his thigh, slowly, carefully.

Will stood up straight. "Keep it. I don't want any part of that money." It burned that he'd ever given his friends reason to think he was the kind of man who might accept it. Soon enough, details of the interview would spread, and everything he was preaching in this parking lot would be outed as pure hypocrisy, anyhow. "But if anything else gets leaked about Leigh, I'll be on you so fast…"

"I would never have done this if it wasn't important," Rex said. "I need this job."

"Never again," he warned.

"Nah, man. Never again. I swear."

Will nodded. His mind was already drifting, his anger fading, only to be replaced by the horror of his own situation, of what Leigh must think of him, and how he'd hurt her. No good would come of incriminating Rex. It wouldn't fix anything, wouldn't undo what Will himself had done. Time to get off his high horse and drop to his knees.

He had a hell of a lot of forgiveness to beg for.

11

THE FINAL MOMENTS of the interview came and went, but Leigh had no clue what she said, surely just a stream of cordial gibberish. When the satellite link was disconnected, she felt more alone than she ever had in her life.

She'd never experienced pain like this. Not even when she'd spoken to Dan the morning of her wedding. This hurt far more, because there was no relief to be found amid the rubble. One minute she'd been in love with a man, and the next that love was wrenched away, sudden as a slap. Early that afternoon she'd been reveling in the sweet soreness that lingered from the previous night's lovemaking, and now... A different hurt. Different by light-years.

Her phone rang, the only number she wanted to see. If ever she'd needed her manager, it was now.

"Angela, hang on." She took her phone to her bedroom, out of earshot of the people disassembling the video equipment. She closed the door and sat on her bed. "Did you watch?"

"Of course I did." Angela's tone belied her hectic job—she was always calm, always soothing. "Leigh, I wish you'd told me the extent of what's going on. Why did you keep that from me, that you were having a fling? And a fling with a guy who'd agreed to report on you?"

The sobs she'd held in for the duration of the interview surged and erupted, leaving her voice broken and thick. "I didn't know he had. I didn't know he was the one who sold the stuff about the party until Jen Landis told me just now. And I didn't think anybody would have pictures of us, together like that. I honestly thought it was a secret."

"He obviously tipped someone off to get them."

She remembered how he'd stepped in so smoothly with that idea to go fishing. How long had Will spent hatching that seemingly spontaneous idea, coordinating with some unknown photographer? How close might he have come to selling something far more intimate, in details or photos? Suddenly, Leigh's heartbreak trickled away nearly to nothing, making room for more anger than she'd known herself capable of feeling.

Angela sighed. "Considering what a curveball that was, you did brilliantly."

"No, I didn't. I bet everybody watching could tell I had no clue about him selling that story."

"I think you're okay. I think it was clear, and rather charmingly so, that you didn't want your affair to be public. And that's good. We don't want you coming off as having staged all this for attention. Not on top of you running off last weekend. And you didn't lie about anything."

"Except messing around with…" She trailed off.

"No one can blame you for omitting that, wanting to be discreet. And you handled the Dan questions perfectly. If he keeps returning the favor, I think all that unpleasantness can fade into obscurity in a few months. But what I want to talk to you about is how you're going to confront this Burgess guy. *If* you're going to confront him."

Leigh considered that. "Part of me doesn't want to see him ever again, but another part wants answers. I don't know. And

I don't know what he might tell the press, depending on how I confront him."

"Exactly. I think we ought to offer to buy his silence."

Leigh imagined that moment, making that offer. She imagined Will agreeing with a stoic nod, confirming that all she'd ever been to him was a payday. Nearly two paydays, if she'd been idiotic enough to give him money for his stupid club. Was it even *for* a club? How much of a con man was Will Burgess, exactly?

"Leigh?"

"I'm thinking."

"It's the best solution, in my opinion. I know it sucks, that he lied to you—"

"I liked him so much, Angela. I feel like such a… I don't know. I feel so stupid. I thought he liked me, too, just for who I am."

"I hate to say it, but this sort of thing happens all the time."

Leigh sighed. "I know."

"It's hard in this business, to know who your friends and lovers really are. It takes a long time to build trust with a person who's from the outside."

"It must. I was with Dan for two years and even then…" She stopped herself, not ready to suffer two open wounds at once.

"Honestly, as unfair as it feels, the tidiest thing is for us to pay him off in exchange for his word that he won't communicate with anyone about any of this. I'm happy to get all of that in motion, if you have his number."

"I don't. I always just walked to his place." She pictured that stretch of beach, where so many wonderful memories had been forged in so short a time. All the beauty had drained out of this place. "I need to come home. As soon as possible."

"I'll get you out on a flight tomorrow."

A horrible thought struck her. "Oh, God, he's the only person who can fly me to the mainland."

"No, Leigh, I'll figure something out with the resort. I'll find another private charter to take you. And failing that, if you really can't stand to see him, we'll get you out on a boat, okay?"

She took a deep breath. "Yeah, okay. Thanks."

"For now I'm going to get in touch with the staff and hunt this guy's number down. I'm also going to consult with the rest of the team and decide how we ought to spin this debacle, once you're home. You're probably going to need to do a follow-up interview or two, if only to solidify the fact that this thing with Burgess was just a fling. We don't need him getting elevated to press-worthy himself."

"No, definitely not."

"So my advice to you is to lie low. Get yourself packed, try to stay calm, and don't go after him, please. If he comes to you—which I'll make plain you don't want him to do—tell him you don't want to talk to him. Do you think you need any protection? I'm sure I could have the resort send someone. Though if he's going to lose his job, I'd prefer for all of that to go down after you've left."

"I'm not afraid of him."

"Good. I'm going to start on these calls, if you don't need me for anything else immediately."

"I'm still in shock. I don't know what to think or feel yet."

"Understandably. Just don't do anything rash, okay? Just pack, and breathe, and don't talk to anyone but me. And your folks, if you're up to it." Angela could appreciate that Leigh's parents didn't always make matters simpler. "I'll call you as soon as I have updates."

They said goodbye and the awful feelings returned, the echoing dread and hurt. The phone chimed, her mother's tone, and Leigh ignored it. She'd stick solely with Angela's guidance for now. She let the tears flow, hot streaks slipping down her burning cheeks.

She replayed her first meeting with Will, scanning it for signs of what was to come, his real intentions. He'd questioned her very little, just a couple cursory queries about why'd she'd run out on her wedding day. He'd insisted on taking her to her villa himself, but again, he hadn't pried. But that was no exoneration—he was just gifted at playing the long game. He was a good-looking man, and charming in his own abrasive way. He'd probably been conning women for years, and had known she'd fall for him. The personal tidbits he'd gotten out of her she'd offered freely. She'd thought they'd traded those intimate details, about her heartbreak, his father's illness. Was his dad even sick? Was he even a cab driver?

Leigh froze.

Will knew about Dan cheating on her. He was the only outsider who knew.

But did that really matter? He could command a steep fee—a bribe, no less—to keep his mouth shut on that topic, but even if it did get out, what was the worst outcome? Leigh was already humiliated. Dan was the one who stood to take the real heat, Leigh having proved she was content to keep the matter private. She'd be another sad celebrity on the receiving end of a high profile betrayal, and a fool for falling for a stranger hired to snoop on her. That'd make her gullible and naive, pitiable, but at least none of her crimes of character were malicious.

She sighed, letting a measure of her angst go. Looking around the room, she settled into what had to be done. Get packed, wait for any updates from Angela. Just like that, Leigh was back where she always had been, adrift in the momentum of her life.

AN HOUR AND A HALF AFTER speaking with Rex, Will turned off his phone. He hadn't made it past the parking lot, sit-

ting on the open tailgate of his truck, fielding calls. Another
from Jackie, in full panic mode. Then one call from L.A.,
from Leigh's manager or publicist or someone. Thank goodness his father didn't know yet…though it was only a matter
of time before one of Will's aunts or cousins heard the story
and passed it along.

He should be feeling something. Shock or horror. He
should be doing something, but he had no idea what that
something was.

He'd just been offered thousands of dollars by Leigh's management agency. He'd cobbled together the gist of the TV interview from all the calls. There were photos of them, on the
beach. Leigh had pretended to know he'd been in bed with
the tabloids, to save face, and now, of course, she really did
know. She thought he'd only ever been after the money, and
her PR team seemed positive he was planning to sell juicier
details about their affair.

He had repeated the same thing, over and over. He didn't
want the money. He'd backed out of the deal. He'd never meant
for things to go this far. But all he got in return were assurances of a payoff, one that had ballooned from five grand to
fifteen and well beyond, the longer he refused it.

"It's best for everyone involved that you leave Miss Bailey
alone," had been the last word from her side.

But he couldn't do that. He'd heard everyone's feelings
except Leigh's, and hers were the only ones that mattered
to him.

No need to ditch his truck at home this time—their in-
volvement was far from private now. He parked in the drive-
way, shaking and dry-mouthed as he mounted her front steps
and pressed the bell. How many times had he stood here
in the last few days, filled with excitement? The dread and
shame that filled him now were leaden, threatening to sink
him straight through the sand and bury him alive.

He caught sight of her through the window, across the living room at the threshold of her bedroom, a shopping bag in her hand. She was still dressed in her interview clothes. They locked eyes, then she promptly closed the door. Will jogged around to the back patio. She spotted him through the glass wall as she set her bag on the bed, and crossed her arms over her chest. As he neared, she shook her head, her face stony.

"Leigh, I need to talk to you."

She turned away and left the bedroom. Will tried the door, but found it predictably locked. "Leigh, please!"

He'd just humiliated her on television, maybe even broken her heart, if their feelings were as mutual as he'd hoped only this morning. Intentional or not, he'd done all that, and he couldn't harass her on top of it…but neither could he give up. He banged on the glass, shouting a last-ditch plea.

"Leigh! We have to talk. I'll be on the beach when you're ready."

He walked down to the shore and sat facing the water. He'd wait as long as he had to. As long as it took for her to come out, or to call Reception and have him physically removed. He owed her far more than patience, and he'd sit out here until the sun was bleaching his bare bones, if that's what it took.

LEIGH CHECKED HER PHONE. Ten o'clock, and Will was still sitting on her beach. From the dark bedroom, she could just make him out in the moonlight, and she shook her head at his tenacity. Then again, she could have called and asked to have him escorted away hours ago.

Did she want to talk to him, or merely to know he was out there, suffering? The former, she finally admitted to herself. She didn't want assurances he cared about her—she'd never be able to believe him, anyhow. But she did want the truth. She wanted to know why he'd hurt her.

Just before eleven, she slid the patio door open and shivered in the cool night air. She crossed the sand silently, and before she announced her presence, she studied him. His strong arms were wrapped around his bent knees, his eyes fixed on the dark sea. That capable body looked broken, his energy gone from vibrant to despairing.

Yes, Will Burgess was a very good actor. Better than Leigh could ever hope to be.

She kicked sand at his leg and he snapped into action, scrambling to his feet.

"Leigh."

"Sit," she said, and took a seat herself, hugging her legs.

Will sat and his mouth opened and closed two or three times. He smiled weakly, clearly at a loss. "I don't know what to say to—"

"You don't know what to say?" She laughed. "You better figure something out, because I only came out to hear whatever pathetic justifications you might have for lying to me."

Again his lips parted, but nothing emerged.

"You've been sitting here for five hours and didn't rehearse a grand speech? A farewell performance?"

"I never lied to you, Leigh."

"No? You kept a pretty straight face when that first story broke. No clue who leaked that to the press, huh? Then the photos?" It hurt to even look at him, this handsome man who'd gone from heady crush to gigantic mistake so quickly. So publicly.

"I didn't tell them a thing. And I didn't take those pictures. How could I have?"

"But you told someone else to. You knew you'd take me fishing that morning. You could have easily tipped someone off."

"I didn't have a thing to do with it, I swear." He drew a deep breath before looking her square in the eyes. "But I did talk to the press, before you came here. I agreed to help them, but I never did. I backed out."

For a long moment, neither spoke, then he said, "I'm sorry I hurt you."

The words stung. She didn't want him knowing he'd hurt her, that she cared. But anyone could've seen the affection she'd beamed at him those fleeting, blissful nights. Anyone could guess what a moron she felt like now.

"How could you have let things go as far as they did, knowing I felt something for you?"

"I felt it, too."

She made a disgusted noise, shaking her head.

"I was never with you for the story. I never planned to get close to you. All I thought it would be was chatting with you, on the plane, selling a few innocent details. Nothing ugly. Nothing personal. I never went digging for dirt."

"But I'm sure you gave yourself a big high five every time I dropped some in your lap."

"No, I didn't. Once we talked at the party, I knew I couldn't go through with it. I told the tabloid editor to fuck off that same night. That's what I meant when I told you my gig fell through."

"Maybe," she said, nodding. "Maybe that's true. Maybe the second you realized you could sleep with me. Maybe right then, you decided you couldn't take the money."

"That's not fair."

"Don't tell me what's fair and what's not. You're always just the right price away from selling your ethics, aren't you? A bribe or an extra paycheck or an invitation into some-body's bed. I bet right now you're wishing you stuck with the money." She huffed a breath. "You *slept* with me. What were you hoping to buy when you auctioned off the details on that one? Your own island?"

"I never—"

"Tell me, Will, am I going to discover in a week's time that I've joined the celebrity sex-tape club?"

Her eyes had adjusted to the dark and she could see when his face fell, utterly. "Oh, Leigh. Jesus, no. Like I said, I told them to screw off the second I got to know you. The second I realized I was in danger of having feelings for you—"

She shot to her feet, cutting off his reply. "I don't know what I came out here expecting to hear. And I don't care what your excuses are. I just know I've spent the last ten years desperately trying to stay sane and respectable." She dusted the sand from her legs, not meeting his eyes. "Coming here the way I did, that was my own fault. But this… Well, all this is my fault, too. For trusting a man I barely knew, and for not having the good sense to expect that this is exactly what would happen." She should have known this was the only way it could have ended. Not like those stupid movies. If only everything had faded to black, credits rolling just after they kissed on the beach…

Will stood. "Leigh—"

"Enjoy whatever justifications let you sleep at night, but spare me, please. All you are to me now is a mistake, one I should have seen coming a mile away. I screwed up, trusting you and telling you so much. I screwed up when I slept with you, and when I fell for you. Because I did. I don't care if that makes you feel like a shit or a huge frigging stud. I can only control how it makes *me* feel, which is disappointed. But I'll get over it. You were a hard, ugly lesson to learn, Will Burgess. And I hope I forget about you as soon as possible."

"Leigh—"

"I know you haven't accepted my manager's deal, by the way."

"Of course I didn't."

"I can only assume it's because you're holding out for more, or because you think you can get a bigger payoff from the press if you tell them everything you know. And you know…" She felt the tears again, the heat rising in her face. "You know what happened the morning of my wedding. The worst day of my life." *Second* worst day of her life.

Will kept his mouth shut, holding her gaze in the near dark.

"We both know you could sell the story. But if any of what you've said to me tonight is true, prove it by at least keeping your mouth shut about that. Everything that happened between us was my mistake, and your secret to blab to whoever wants to cut you the fattest check. But that stuff about me and Dan isn't yours."

"I'm not going to tell anyone anything. Especially not that."

"I'll believe it when I see it." She started to turn away, then stopped. "And if you really do have a sick father, I hope he gets better. And I hope your club is successful, so you won't wake up and realize you got his hopes up for nothing, like you did mine. If karma doesn't come back to bite you in the ass, I hope you're goddamn grateful for whatever you get from jerking me around."

Despite the persisting misery, Leigh felt lighter as she turned and headed toward the patio. She'd said everything she needed to, and she'd leave here tomorrow with no regrets regarding how she'd handled things.

She felt sand hit the backs of her calves as Will jogged to catch up.

"Leigh, I have no idea what to say to make you believe me."

"That makes two of us."

"Even when I first took the offer and we were total strangers, I never wanted to hurt you. I could have told them any number of things about what happened between us, and I didn't."

"You couldn't. I'd have known it was you."

"No, that's not why."

"Spare me, Will."

"I didn't—"

She whirled toward him. "Don't. Just don't. Even if you did refuse that paycheck, even if you did feel bad about it, how could you have accepted my offer of money without coming clean?"

Will's expression changed, and when he spoke his voice was soft and quiet. "I didn't want to lose you."

"Lose my money, you mean."

"No, you. I couldn't stand the idea of hurting you. And not just because of how guilty I'd feel. Because I knew how much it meant to you, feeling like a normal person here and being taken at face value. And that *is* how I felt about you, as soon as I got to know you. I just wanted the mistake I made to go away, like it had never happened. You deserved to feel that what we had was real."

"I deserved to live a lie? I deserved to sleep with a man who was being paid to get dirt on me, and believe it was what I so badly wanted it to be?"

"No, it wasn't a lie. Everything that happened between us was real to me. The second I felt something for you, I called it off."

She shook her head. "All that tells me is that you value sex *slightly* more than money. You may be ethical enough to know you can't take both, but that doesn't make you a good person. It sure as hell doesn't make you into the man I thought I was falling in love with."

That shut him up. They stared at one another for a few seconds, and when Leigh walked away, she knew he wasn't following.

She entered her villa through the bedroom, locked the door. She went to the living room and sifted through freshly missed calls and messages, and after ten minutes or more, she heard Will's truck start up and drive away.

She dropped her head into her palms. She prayed he'd take

Angela's buyout over what the press might offer him. How pathetic that she'd fallen for Will, thinking him the antithesis of Hollywood duplicity. She'd have given him that money gladly. She'd practically begged him to let her, and she'd bought his hesitation. Now he'd get that and more, from her or the tabloids. He nearly deserved it—he'd played her like a fiddle.

But he'd hurt far more than her bank account or her pride. He'd wrecked her hope that she'd ever find true love, a man who loved her for who she really was. For a few glorious days she thought she'd found that, but it had been an illusion, as phoney as a movie set.

Whatever profit came to Will for all her heartbreak, she hoped it was saddled with a steep tax of guilt. But more than that, she wanted him punished, she wanted him gone. Rounded up with all the other regrets of the past ten years, packed away and left to collect dust while she moved on. Living one's life well was said to be the best revenge, and Leigh would do just that. And if she never thought about Will Burgess again, she'd be halfway there.

AN EXCEEDINGLY UNWELCOME sight greeted Will as he arrived at the dock the next morning. Twenty feet from his own plane was another one. Bigger, newer, certainly more expensive, and splashed with the logo of a charter company that served islands off the southern coast of Barbados. He strode into the reception area. He was bound to get fired sooner or later. No point putting it off.

There was indeed a strange pilot loitering by the front desk, chatting with the receptionist and the day manager, Analee. His uniform was crisp, its patches more for show than to tout any actual accomplishment, Will decided. He walked over, faking cheer.

"Morning, ladies."

Analee nodded curtly, with nothing like her usual warm demeanor. "Captain."

"This my replacement?" Will aimed a thumb in the stranger's direction.

Analee crossed her arms over her imposing bosom. "No. There's a special charter this morning. You're still the pilot 'round here."

For now. "Special charter?"

"One of the guests requested it."

The pilot stepped forward and offered a hand and an introduction, which Will returned grudgingly.

He bade them goodbye, panic rising in his chest as he exited. Leigh had requested this asshole, no doubt. What had Will expected? That she'd stick out the rest of her honeymoon after he broke her heart? The resort would surely be comping her stay, to make up for what had happened. Even if they did value Will's service enough to overlook his nearly getting in bed with a tabloid—for that matter, a guest—they'd be garnisheeing his wages for years to recoup the loss. Though it was far more likely he'd be fired as soon as the gossip dust settled and they had all the facts straight.

It burned. These people had been Will's family for the better half of a decade, and he'd let everyone down. Let himself down. Let Leigh down, which tied for the lowest low right beside letting his dad down.

But now wasn't the time for regret. This was the last chance he'd have to talk to Leigh before she flew out of his life for good.

LEIGH'S CAR ARRIVED at ten-thirty sharp. The driver helped her with her suitcases and she bade a goodbye to the villa, a week sooner than planned. It wasn't a good riddance…not quite. Though the memories she'd made here with Will had withered from roses to ash, she'd also gotten a lot figured out about herself within these walls and on the surrounding sand. She was bruised, but she'd started to feel like herself again, for the first time in years.

Sleep hadn't arrived the previous night, and she hoped once she was on a flight back to Los Angeles it might catch up with her. Though more likely, somebody would recognize her between Bridgetown and LAX, throw her off balance and she'd be back to square one. Such was the price of living in reality.

Sadly, she was doomed to be thrown off balance before even leaving Harrier Key. Will's plane should have been long gone for the mainland, but she spotted it from the parking lot. And as the hired pilot escorted Leigh and her bags from the car, she found Will himself waiting halfway down the dock, arms locked over his chest.

"Make way kindly, Captain," Leigh's new pilot said as they approached.

"Just need to talk to Miss Bailey."

"I don't want to talk to you," she said over her escort's shoulder. "You had your chance to say what you needed to last night, and that's more than I owed you."

Will's posture changed once he was speaking to her, not the pilot. His shoulders sank and his face went from set to pained. "I don't even want to talk, Leigh. I want to know what I can do to fix this."

"Make way," the new pilot repeated, beginning to crowd Will. He stepped to the edge of the dock, letting them pass, then followed.

"Leigh, tell me what I can do."

"You've already done plenty. More than enough, in fact."

"Tell me how to make this up to you."

She stopped to glare at him, both stopping in their tracks. "By leaving me alone." His expression gave her the tiniest pause, that same broken glimmer she'd seen when he spoke about his father's situation. Too bad for him, she wasn't ready to believe it was anything more than another tool in his manipulative arsenal. "Just stay out of my life."

She turned to catch up with the new pilot.

"I'm in love with you, Leigh."

She froze. For a long moment she stared at her feet, at the water glinting between the aluminum slats. Heat was rising through her like steam. No, lava. Her fists shook as she turned to glare daggers at him.

"Leigh—"

"How *dare* you say that." Two years hadn't been enough for Dan to truly love her. How would Will claim to feel the same after a single *week*?

"It's true."

She closed the ten-foot gap between them, marching right up to give him a sharp shove in the chest. It sent him back a pace, nowhere near enough to knock him on his butt or send him toppling into the waves. But for deferring little people-pleaser Leigh Bailey, it was a full-on assault. Oddly enough, it was herself that Leigh wanted to knock some sense into, because for better or worse, she'd fallen in love with Will. Just as quickly, and far more foolishly.

"You don't love me. You barely know me."

Will paused a beat or two before saying simply, "I love you, anyway."

"Live in that delusion if it makes you feel better, but it won't change the fact that you don't respect me. Not my privacy or my feelings or my space even, coming here like this. You just love yourself, and you can't stand letting me leave thinking badly of you."

"You know that's not true." Sure, he'd never seemed too worried about her opinion of his character when they'd first met. But still.

"Love me all you want. But I can't wait to get home and

forget about you. If you loved me—if you *respected* me—you'd leave me alone to do just that. So that's how you make this up to me, Will Burgess. You keep standing right there and let me make my getaway."

His blue eyes were full of defeat. He didn't speak, didn't follow. When Leigh's plane took off he was right where she'd left him on the dock, standing with his hands in his pockets. He didn't wave as the craft banked and charted a course for Bridgetown. Leigh watched him fade until he was just another speck, another anonymous shape to leave behind with the rest of her disastrous honeymoon.

12

THE FIRST WEEK BACK HOME was the worst. The meetings were endless; daily meetings with Angela and the other members of the PR team. Meetings with friends who'd excitedly bought new dresses and gifts for Leigh's wedding and deserved some answers.

But things slowly quieted down. Leigh submitted to a second interview, with a respectable fashion and lifestyle magazine. She let them do an editorial photo shoot centered around her holding billowing swathes of gauzy fabric before a wind machine on the beach, a metaphor about her newfound freedom or some such stylish nonsense. More designed to sell the summer's hot trends, but what the hell, it was fun. And the interviewer let Leigh focus mainly on her future plans instead of the details of her split with Dan or her rebound with...

Sigh.

As for Dan himself, he'd stayed dutifully mum and cordial, with not a single snide sentiment to share on the topic of Leigh's rather quick recasting of his role in their honeymoon. Her things had been carefully boxed and labeled and were waiting at her parents' house, the paperwork to remove her name from their condo drawn up and ready to sign, her half of the money waiting to be transferred. Dan was as fair and sensitive as always, which let Leigh forgive herself for having loved him once. Their wedding day may have proved the most expensive breakup in history, but as the days went on, that's what it was beginning to feel like. A breakup, no longer a crisis. Her friends would forgive her. All she needed was time and patience and humility, and things would be okay.

Crashing with her parents felt comforting for a few days, but once things settled down, she found herself back amid their endless bickering. Bickering over Leigh's choices, Leigh's career, Leigh's future. All these years and she was still their smoke screen. But let them waste their energy on it, if it was what they loved so much. Leigh had her own decisions to make now, whether they approved or not.

Step one, *figure out what to do with my life*. Hell of a step. She renumbered it as step two, and made finding a temporary apartment across town her first priority.

Though she'd hoped she'd left him behind on that dock, Leigh hadn't forgotten about Will Burgess. Or what he'd said when they parted. Each day that passed with no fresh gossip leaked about their affair dulled Leigh's pain. Her guard was still up, but after two weeks' dead silence from Will, she'd begun to let herself feel optimistic.

A more famous actress's epic meltdown had overshadowed Leigh's boring old flight-and-fling, and though her and Will's story was disappearing from the Hollywood blogs, her memories of him weren't.

Troublingly, she thought less and less about how he'd hurt her, and more and more about the fun and passionate moments they'd shared. If he never told the press another thing about her, she'd probably be able to forgive him. She might be able to believe that he hadn't conned her on purpose, that their romance had been the real deal....

She hoped so. It had felt wonderful, loving someone that way. It was ruined with Will, but it heartened her to know she had the potential inside her, that she might be able to recapture that ecstatic, easy feeling with another man. Someday.

It was a week later when Will suddenly burst back into her life, in the last place she'd expected.

Leigh was flipping through magazines in the waiting room of her accountant's office, twenty minutes early for her appointment. The agency handled entertainers' finances almost exclusively, and communal narcissism dictated that the television set into the wall be tuned to the Hollywood news channel. The current show had been nothing more than a background drone to Leigh until it returned from a commercial, and her chin jerked up at the sound of her name.

"Anyone wondering what became of Leigh Bailey's hunky honeymoon rebound?"

"Oh, dear God." She craned her neck and found the secretary on the phone, no chance of asking for the remote to turn this nonsense off. Leigh looked back to the screen, groaning at the splashy graphic; Will's handsome face above the obnoxious title Pilots of the Caribbean!

"We caught up with Captain William Burgess in Bridgetown, Barbados. Here's Erin with the latest."

The scene changed to a perky young reporter approaching Will. He was on the beach, busy with a hacksaw and a stack of two-by-fours. Leigh cursed her middle for fluttering the way it did. Traitor.

"Captain Burgess?"

Will stood, frowning, and set down his saw. *"Yeah."*

"Erin Mayfair, with The Daily Dish.*"*

"Whatever you ask, the answer is 'no comment.'"

The segment was edited, jumping ahead to Will standing a bit closer, a microphone in his face, his resistance apparently worn down. Goddamn those eyes. Blue as real life in high definition.

"Do you regret how things ended with Leigh Bailey?"

"Leigh's a lovely woman. I'm sure she's doing just fine."

"Word has it your deal with the papers fell through and you had to sell your plane to buy this property."

The flutter in Leigh's stomach collapsed to a lurch.

A grim smile from Will. *"Any deal I was offered, I refused. And yeah, I sold my plane. You think I'd be doing this myself if I could afford a crew?"*

Shows like this were geniuses at telling you who to like and who to hate, and the audience was clearly meant to hate Will. His appeal was an acquired taste, and although it worked well enough in person, he came off like a snarky jackass on TV. Leigh felt another funny pang in her middle, and realized she'd forgiven Will enough to feel badly for him.

"And what exactly are you working on, Captain?"

He nodded to the building behind him, and the camera panned. It was that derelict old property, just as Leigh remembered it, only infinitely less personal on screen. *"Bit of renovation."* No plug for the club. No grasping for media pity by explaining about his father.

"What else has been going on in your life since Leigh left for the States? Any love interests to report?"

Will blinked at the camera. *"I don't seriously qualify as a celebrity, do I? You people don't seriously care if some nobody who once crossed paths with a vacationing actress is dating or not, do you? Can I have my own show?"*

Having painted Will as a jerk, the reporter turned to the camera. *"Erin Mayfair, Bridgetown, Barbados."*

Leigh shook her head and a segment about Hollywood slimming secrets came on. She fished her phone from her bag and dialed Angela.

"Hey, Leigh. What can I do for you?"

"You weren't watching the entertainment news just now, were you?"

A pause, then Angela's voice returned, cold with dread. "No. Why?"

"Don't panic, nothing too terrible. But I thought it might've given you a laugh. They had Will Burgess on. He didn't fare so hot."

"No, I don't imagine a man of his...*charms* would come off well with the press. Glad you sound okay about it, though. Does this mean your pride's officially on the mend?"

"I think so. I sure as heck hope so."

"Good. I've actually been sitting on some Burgess news of my own for a couple days, thinking I ought to wait until I knew you could bear hearing his name."

"Oh, what kind of news?"

Angela laughed. "My turn to tell *you* not to panic. It's good news—he's finally agreed to a buyout offer. Of his own design."

Leigh cringed, not liking the sound of that. A fresh knife in the heart, after she'd just mustered sympathy for the man. She sighed. "Go on."

"He agreed to sign papers promising never to speak about your relationship, or you personally, on one condition. That condition being that I quit offering him money for it and never call him again."

Leigh felt her brow furrow. "I see."

"If I'd known his price really was zero dollars, I'd have quit ramping the offer up by five grand every time I called him. I was tempted to tell you the day it happened, but I thought it'd be kind to give you a little more time."

So he'd told her the truth about what he planned to do with what he knew.... Hell, now she had no clue what to make of him.

"One other thing, Leigh, since you brought the guy up."

"What?"

"I've got a package from him, at the office."

"Oh. What was it?"

"I don't know. It's addressed to you. Should I have it dropped off?"

Leigh chewed her lip. How bad could it be? Well, it could be really bad, actually. Could be more photos or some secret sex tape, evidence he thought it was kind to surrender to her, though knowing he'd ever done such a thing would destroy her all over again. But what the hell. Being destroyed—twice in one month, no less—had made her stronger in the greater scheme of things. "Yeah, fine. Send it over."

Her accountant appeared from the hallway. "Sorry, Angela, I have an appointment to go to," Leigh said.

"No worries. Glad for a chance to bring you up-to-speed. And please let me know what's in this mysterious box when you get it. We've got a little pool going here in the office. My money's on a big wad of Barbadian cash, to make up for ruining your luxury vacation. Most of the girls say if it's anything short of his heart on ice, it's not enough."

"I'm not interested in either of those things. But I'll call you later and solve the mystery for everyone."

They said goodbye and Leigh headed into her appointment, curious to discuss the options for her finances, the options for her future. Whatever lay ahead, it was bound to be better than the way she'd been floundering for the past few years. And even if she drove herself into a ditch, finally steering her own life… Well, at least it'd be her hands on the wheel for a change.

LEIGH'S HEAD WAS SPINNING by the time she got back home, late that afternoon. She'd been presented with a virtual buffet of options for what to do with her money, and as exciting as it all was, she felt punch-drunk and overwhelmed. College? But to become what? More investments? Fund a business? Perhaps, but she wanted such a decision to feel personal, more than an investment of her savings. Rather, an investment of her excitement and energy and faith, and she didn't know where such things ought to be directed just yet.

She was so overloaded she'd completely forgotten about the package.

The box, only as big as a brick, had been signed for by the doorman and left in her mailbox. Leigh brought it into her apartment, sitting on the couch with it. She peeled off the courier service's slip and studied the address label. Funny how she could've felt so close to Will and not even known what his handwriting looked like.

She grabbed a pen from her bag and slit open the tape. As she pulled crumpled newspaper from the box, something rolled out and onto the cushions. A peanut butter jar. Leigh laughed, more surprised than amused. It had been emptied and cleaned, and she unscrewed the lid to discover a wad of tissue paper and a curled-up card—a postcard.

Sliding out the latter, she found a note taped to its edge. She flattened it against her leg and studied the glossy image, a sunset on a Caribbean shore, with Bridgetown set in fancy script along the bottom. Just a silly photo of a beach she'd never been to, but there she was again, in her mind's eye, sitting on that warm white sand, drunk on all those colors.... Holding her breath, she flipped the postcard over. Will's writing took up the entire back, growing smaller and smaller as he'd filled the space, then continuing on the attached notepaper.

Leigh,
You asked me to leave you alone, so let me preface this first and foremost with a fresh apology. It was selfish of me to make contact, though I suspect my selfishness won't surprise you. But still, I'm sorry.
I have no doubt that you won't deem me worthy of in-

dulging in your precious peanut butter therapy, so I've
sent the tiniest, most inadequate token in its place. I
thought the gift was a wise one. If you don't like it as
it is, you can smash it with a hammer while picturing
my face.

Leigh set the postcard aside and upended the jar, dropping
the tissue-wrapped bundle onto the couch. Her fingers shook
as she peeled the layers away, finding a jewelry box inside.
She took the lid off, and sitting on a pillow of cotton was a
pendant. Smooth glass, big as a domino. Clear, pale blue fading to turquoise, to aqua, to green and citron and yellow, then
finally to opaque cream. A Bajan beach sunset, small enough
to wrap one's hand around. Leigh did just that, squeezing the
glass in her fist as she picked the postcard back up.

I signed some papers for your management agency,
promising to keep my mouth shut, no bribe necessary.
I'm sure that means more than a hunk of pretty glass,
knowing you can sue my pants off if I'm lying. Which
would be tragic, as my pants are about all I've got left.

She recalled what she'd heard on the TV that afternoon.
He'd sold his plane. She remembered, too, what Angela had
said, and realized that Will's severed heart wasn't in this box.
His heart was tethered to a strange owner's dock or locked in
a hangar someplace, someone else's name on the deed, someone else's fingerprints all over the console. Will could've
made that money and more by selling Leigh's secrets, but he
hadn't. He'd traded the thing she'd assumed he valued above
all else—his freedom.

Chest aching, sinuses stinging, Leigh turned back to his
letter.

To tell you I'm sorry may be the truth, but it's also
grossly inadequate. But I am sorry. For ever considering using you at first, and for humiliating you in the
end. You're the last person who deserves that.

But I'm not sorry for what happened in the middle, what
we shared before I wrecked everything, because it was
the closest I've ever felt to a woman, ever in my life.
It sucks beyond comprehension that it might feel like
the opposite to you, nothing but a regret. Or maybe I'm
giving myself too much credit.

If I was a more eloquent man, I'd have come up with
something worth your time to read. But we both know
finesse isn't my strong suit. So all I can do is say it
again—I'm sorry. I'm sorry, and I meant everything I
ever said to you, on the beach and in bed and on that
dock, the day you left. If I manage to meet someone half
as amazing as you in my next thirty-three years, it'll be
more than I deserve. Though for now, I'm still hope-
lessly, helplessly in love with you. It hurts like a bitch,
but I guess that just proves karma's for real.

Best of luck with whatever you decide to do with your
life. I hope you keep dancing. "Plain old Leigh" dancing on the sand is just about the most beautiful thing
I've ever seen, so I hope you let her call the shots from
now on. She won't steer you wrong.

Love (the really painful, torturous kind),
Will

She read the letter again, then set it aside, feeling more
confused than ever, but softened. The knot in her chest had
been slit, and though her edges were still frayed, she could
breathe now. She could think of Will and not feel angry. It
wasn't clear exactly what had settled in to replace the anger,
but it hurt far less.

The pendant had grown warm against her palm and she opened her hand to study it. She'd seen plenty like it, hanging in craft stalls in the Bridgetown tourist district, anyone's for a few dollars. It was just what Will had claimed, a token, but it meant as much as a blue box from Tiffany's, rattling with diamonds. It meant as much as any mere object could—

Leigh sat up straight. With a bolt of illogical, intuitive clarity, she knew something. She knew what her first new investment had to be.

13

ANOTHER GORGEOUS afternoon in paradise.

The sun was shining, the breeze cool, the music playing from Will's radio chirpy and buoyant. Yet he felt like a man apart from all this island cheer, cold in the shadow of his own private cloud cover.

Still, as he surveyed his progress, there was a light glinting at the end of his tunnel.

He downed a liter of water and went back to work, priming the freshly sanded exterior boards he'd replaced.

It was tough, feeling trapped in the middle of this endless project. He had always been built for mobility and whim, not commitment. Harder still was not being able to glance to the water and see *The Passport* bobbing in the waves, promising escape.

But Will's wings had been clipped for weeks now, and the pain was fading in tandem with his fears that the house might never be done. It might not be a serviceable, licensed bar for months, but the wiring was complete, the top floor nearly ready to inhabit.

Technically, Will had been inhabiting it for the last few weeks, if crashing in a sleeping bag counted. The bedrooms' furniture had been delivered and assembled that very morning; the bathroom was finished and the kitchen functional. Will's dad had phoned the previous afternoon to confirm his flight details. One-way ticket to paradise…work-in-progress though paradise might currently be.

The thought put a smile on Will's face, letting him forget the ache in his heart, for a few moments, anyhow.

All those years he'd spent free of guilt and obligations, his life built around avoiding a debt of conscience, each affair and friendship and promise designed with a ready escape hatch… Leigh had flown away and taken all that simplicity with her, and the hole she'd left felt like a physical wound, ragged and stinging. And it was far more than guilt. It was grief, for having stumbled into something that made the emotional investment so unquestionably worth the risk, only to wreck it all.

Will paused to rub the back of his hand across his forehead, cursing the headache brewing there. He dipped the brush into the primer and swiped it down a bare board, each stroke a tiny step toward doing the right thing. Being the sort of man his father was, maybe becoming the sort of man a woman like Leigh deserved to—

"Captain."

He jumped and turned, his world flipping upside down in a breath. "Leigh."

They stood in silence for an endless moment, and Will squinted at her from twenty paces away, hopeful and frightened and confused.

"Are you actually standing there, or have I been breathing paint fumes for too long?"

"Pretty sure I'm standing here. Unless I've been breathing too much L.A. smog." She smiled. "Hi, Will."

"Hi." Snapping awake, he set down his brush and walked to her, stopping a few feet away and fighting every physical instinct he had. He wanted to hug her, to hold her…hell, he'd settle for a handshake, even a slap. Anything to prove she was real, close enough to touch. "What are you doing here?"

"I'm not a hundred percent sure."

"Oh." Stymied, Will glanced around. He spotted the cooler and folding chair in the shade of the building. "Would you like a beer?"

"Um, sure."

He headed for the little break area and opened a bottle for her, waving to invite her to have a seat. Will cracked a beer for himself and leaned again the side of the house. Leigh seemed to settle in, attention on her drink for half a minute before she spoke.

"Thank you," she finally said. "For the agreement you signed, and for keeping quiet. For keeping your promise."

"Oh. Right. You're welcome."

She stared at the sand and grass, stoically sipping, gathering her thoughts. She looked up again and her eyes left Will unable to breathe, dying for whatever words might come next.

"I saw you, on TV," she said. "Someone interviewed you out here."

He shook his head, ruing the memory. "You tell them 'no comment' sixty times, then suddenly you're answering questions."

"I know. It's that or throw a tantrum. Either way, they always get what they want."

"I'm sure they edited me to sound like a royal prick. I bet you weren't too happy to have people think that was the guy you had a fling with."

Leigh shrugged. "I'm done worrying what people think of me. I mostly felt bad for you."

"A bit of public humiliation was the least I deserved."

"I heard you sold your plane."

He winced. "Yeah."

"That must have been really hard."

"It should have been the choice I made months ago, but until you left… It just wasn't an option before. Screwing up the way I did with you put things in perspective."

"Oh?"

"You're right—I loved that plane like a limb, but it's a selfish kind of love. Considering all the sacrifices my dad made for me, growing up, it's only fitting."

"Do you know who bought it?"

He shook his head. "I sold it to a resale dealership. Don't want to know who's got their hands all over it now."

Leigh took a deep drink and addressed his knees. "Anyway. I guess I've come to say I forgive you. And I believe you now, that you never intended to profit off what happened. Between us."

"I'm not sure I deserve that courtesy, certainly not if you flew all the way here to tender it."

"Forgiveness isn't a prize, it's a gift. And I'm choosing to give mine to you."

She set down her bottle and stood, extending her hand. Will wiped his palm on his shorts and gripped it. The handshake went on for some time, and he couldn't translate the exact breed of uncertainty that strained her lovely features. Then she smiled, looking embarrassed, and stepped close to hug him. Will accepted the embrace dumbly, hands hovering behind her back. After a moment the shock left him and he squeezed her tightly. In the warmth of her body and the scent of her hair, he relived every minute they'd spent together. They separated after a few seconds, and the awkwardness in the wake of the hug felt good. Honest and real.

"Wow. I wasn't expecting that."

She smirked. "So pleased to have earned myself a *wow,* for a change."

Will sighed, relieved enough to demand some answers.

"If you're not here to smack me, what exactly are you looking for, Leigh? Why'd you come all this way?"

Her body relaxed visibly, and she shuffled sand around with her foot as she spoke. "I'm looking for a sign about what I'm supposed to do next with my life. I think maybe you're a few steps ahead of me on the journey, so I was hoping for some tips."

"Sorry to disappoint you, but I have no clue what I'm doing beyond getting this place livable for my dad."

"Were the proceeds from your plane enough to get everything done?"

He shook his head. "Not even close. But it was capital enough to secure a loan, and I think if I can get the place looking good, with all the utilities and repairs up to code, I stand a chance at putting together a decent business plan and scoring a bit more funding." He sighed, turning to stare out at the water.

Leigh gave his shoulder a squeeze. "You're not built for debt, are you?"

"Feels awful."

"Like an anchor."

He nodded. "But they call them 'growing pains' for a reason. I feel like shit, so I must be making progress."

The two of them wandered down the beach toward the water, and for a long time they watched the ocean, sipping their beers and shading their eyes from the afternoon sun.

"I got your package," Leigh said.

"I hope I wasn't too out of line, sending that when you asked me to leave you alone."

"It arrived at just the right time, really. And the things you had to say… They were things I needed to hear. And after the dust settled, I *wanted* to hear them, too. So thanks."

"You're more than welcome."

"You know what you said to me," Leigh murmured, "on the dock?"

He turned to her. "That I was in love with you?"

She met his gaze. "Did you really mean that?"

"I meant it then, and it's still true." His chest ached, each and every time he thought of her, of her face when they'd parted. And he thought of her constantly.

Leigh craned her neck to survey the building, and Will sensed she didn't want to discuss his proclamation any further.

"So. Tell me what's been happening in your new life, former Miss Movie Star. Have you been letting plain-old-Leigh call some shots?"

She smiled, her attention still on the house. "I have. And I'm proud to say I've already made my first investment."

"Business? Property?"

"Property, I guess." She dug a folded paper from her back pocket and handed it over. Will unfolded the page and his heart stopped. It was a printout from an auction site, a listing with a photo of *The Passport*. He studied Leigh's impassive face, wondering what this meant—revenge, ransom, or least likely of all, a gift he didn't deserve.

"You bought my plane?"

"I did."

"You planning on getting your license?"

"No. I don't plan on doing anything with it, except keep it in storage until the day you can afford to buy it back."

Emotions bubbled up, gratitude and hope and a surge of humbleness that left him speechless for a minute. "What sort of interest do you have in mind?"

"None. I just knew it must be keeping you up at nights, the thought of some other man getting his hands on your precious baby."

He nodded, but he was still ages from feeling comfortable with the gesture. "I don't deserve that. I've got a hell of a lot of restitution to pay you before I get anywhere *close* to deserving that kindness."

"I'm thinking of it as an investment in my own faith in human goodness."

"That's a lot to bank on a man who hurt you as badly as I did."

She smiled faintly. "Like I said, I forgive you, Will. I can't fault you for being shady. I knew that from the first minute I met you, when you asked me for a bribe."

"Technically, I didn't ask. You offered."

She ignored his teasing. "And I fell in love with you, shadiness and all."

Will's mind went blank at her words, more valuable than any amount of money, than his plans, than his plane.

She went on in his numb silence. "You screwed up, kinda terribly."

He nodded.

"But I don't take it personally anymore. And I believe what you told me, about meaning everything you said to me. Even before you sold your plane and signed those papers, I *wanted* to believe you, but it was too much to hope for, after what my ex did to me. But I think maybe I knew it was true, all along. Then the proof you offered gave me permission to accept it."

"Oh. Good."

She grinned, surely in response to the idiotic look on his face.

"Do you…don't you want to know who it was, who actually reported on you?" He didn't want to throw Rex under the bus, but if she asked Will wouldn't lie. He was relieved when she shook her head.

"I know a lot of people would say I'm a doormat for not wanting them hunted down, same as they'd say about me not dragging my ex over the coals…. But I don't want revenge.

I'll leave all that bitterness to the people who thrive on it. Like my parents. Whoever talked, it doesn't matter. I know it wasn't you, and that's all I care about."

He glanced at her collar then, at the shining edge of the pendant peeking out. Spotting his gaze, she touched the glass. "Thank you for this, too."

"It's not nearly—"

Her fingers on his arm cut him off. "Enough with that. I forgave you already. I didn't come here for more apologies."

"What did you come for, then?"

She rubbed her palms together and looked around the beach. "Well, I'd like to know exactly where I'll be sleeping during this renovation."

"Sleeping?"

"I have a potential investment to make a decision about," she said officiously. "I intend to be very hands-on with the project. In fact, after I check out of my hotel, you can tell me where to dump my suitcase and what I can do to start helping."

Will blinked, too distracted by the happy, hesitant joy rising in his chest to put his thoughts into coherent words. "You can, um… Well, I'll find you something. But let me show you where you can stay, if you're hell-bent on slumming it."

He led her into the gutted building, past the would-be main bar and up the stairs to the second floor. He'd been staying in the room with the widest windows, facing the beach.

Leigh stood in the center of the sunny space, gazing out at the view. "Here's where I say *wow*."

He nodded. "I know. This'll be my dad's room, when he comes down."

She turned to meet Will's eyes. "Do you know when that'll be?"

"Next Sunday."

"Exciting."

"Very. I found a suitable nurse for any unexpected issues, just up the road. But I think the climate alone will do him a world of good."

"I'll bet. Cold, icy New York winters…"

"And sweltering, humid summers, yeah. He's not one to admit being excited about things, but when I talk to him, I can tell he's dying to get down here. Get started enjoying a proper retirement." In between complaints about the hassle of getting his apartment cleaned out and the highway robbery also known as his moving service, the old guy's anticipation had been palpable.

"I'm eager to meet him."

Her deep, genuine smile made Will blush. How was this actually real, this moment? How could she truly be here, saying these things to him?

He crossed the bare floor, nervous as he reached down and took her hand. She welcomed the gesture, showing no misgivings in those rare gray eyes. Will ached to pick up where they'd left off before he wrecked things, but it might be too bold, too soon—

She did it for him, her free hand cupping his jaw, drawing him down to press his mouth to hers. It wasn't like those reckless kisses they'd shared the previous month. This one was slower, savoring. Exploratory, as they each remembered how good they were this way. Leigh pulled away far too soon, but the grin on her face warmed him straight through.

"Just like that?" he asked.

"Just like that. You look surprised," she teased.

"A little. No, very."

"Me, too. I wondered the whole trip here whether we'd ever get back to that place. Now I look at you, and my body doesn't care what my brain thinks is the smart thing to do. I just want things to go back to how they were. If you want that, too."

"Of course I do. And in that case, I won't be a gentleman and offer to move my stuff into the smaller room."

Her grin deepened and she bit her lip. "No, please don't. That gives us, what? Nine days to play honeymoon before we lose the luxury suite?" She sent another teasing glance around the room, but Will's brain was stuck on "honeymoon."

"I've been so focused on the business renovations, the living quarters could use a woman's touch. That could be your project, if you like."

"I was more looking forward to some real dirty work, sanding and painting and hammering stuff."

"There's plenty of that to go around."

She straightened, looking him right in the eyes. "I don't honestly know what'll happen, as far as my investing in this bar goes."

"I understand. I'm not sure how comfortable I am with the prospect. Not yet, at least. And I'm in okay shape, since the loan was approved. Hell, who knows—maybe in forty years I'll turn enough of a profit to buy my plane back from you."

She laughed. "Until then, you're welcome to borrow it. Just don't get any smudges on my dials."

He rolled his eyes but smiled, too happy to pretend annoyance. "You're really willing to give this another try? You and me?"

"If you want me. Yeah, I am."

He shook his head at such a ridiculous notion. "If I want you? Jesus, woman. Come here."

She stepped close and he kissed her, deeply and fiercely, vowing to himself to never give her any reason to doubt his feelings, ever again. He released her. "I owe you some hearty wooing. And likely a few nights of dancing, before my dad lands."

Leigh nodded in approval. "Yes, that would be in order."

He glanced at the water through the window. "Come with me."

"Where?"

"Humor me." He took her hand and led her down the steps, across the sand to the ocean's edge, coaxing her to sit. He took a seat behind her, hugging his arms around her waist, chin on her shoulder. The smell of the sea and her skin, her body exactly where he wanted it, pressed warmly to his… "I just want to be like this, for a little while. I'm still trying to wrap my head around the fact that I didn't wreck this."

She leaned into him, heaven on earth. Will kissed her neck, her jaw, her cheek. He'd never have guessed they'd fall back into this, so quickly. So easily.

"You still worried you're drifting?" he asked her. "Just waking up places, not knowing how you got there?"

She shook her head. "Not this time. *Everybody* tried to talk me out of this. My accountant, my manager. My mother more than anybody, and if she couldn't manage to change my mind, nobody can. It just feels right, in my gut. And my heart. I know you hate that feeling, but really—just tie me down. Drop anchor. This is where I'm supposed to be."

"What if you decide you want to drift away again, to follow your own dreams? Go to school? Go to Europe or who knows where?"

"Maybe I will. Who ever knows that sort of thing? But I do know this—I'll be back."

Like the tide, Will thought.

"It feels right, here. The pace of things, and how much smaller I feel. In a good way. The world feels quieter, you know? I like that. But mainly…" She trailed off, and Will waited patiently for her to assemble her thoughts. "It's you. I'm here because of you. To enjoy being caught up in someone else's orbit, for a change."

He watched the sun sinking lower on the horizon, letting

her words linger, letting hope settle down around them, the sensation as sweet and comforting as her body pressed to his. He brushed his lips against her temple, the faintest kiss.

"I love you, Leigh. Way more than I ever knew I was capable of."

"I love you. Way more than I used to think was wise… until I figured out that love and logic have nothing to do with each other."

"Thank goodness for that. I wouldn't stand a chance if you were in your right mind."

"Keep driving me crazy, then. You're good at that."

He smiled, his cheek pressed to hers. "Nothing on earth I'd rather do."

* * * * *

COMING NEXT MONTH FROM

HARLEQUIN® BLAZE™

Available January 22, 2012

#735 THE ARRANGEMENT
by Stephanie Bond

Ben Winter and Carrie Cassidy have known each other forever. And they like each other—a lot! But when those feelings start to run deeper, Ben thinks he's doing the right thing when he ends the "Friends with Benefits" arrangement he has with Carrie. After all, he wants more from her than just great sex. It seems like a good plan...until Carrie makes him agree to find his replacement!

#736 YOU'RE STILL THE ONE • *Made in Montana*
by Debbi Rawlins

Reluctant dude-ranch manager Rachel McAllister hasn't seen Matt Gunderson since he left town and broke her teenage heart ten years ago. Now the bull-riding rodeo star is back and she's ready to show him *everything* he missed. All she wants is his body, but if there's one thing Matt learned in the rodeo, it's how to hang on tight.

HB0113CNMENHA

#737 NIGHT DRIVING • *Stop the Wedding!*
by Lori Wilde

Former G.I. Boone Toliver has a new mission: prevent his kid sister's whirlwind wedding in Miami. The challenge: Boone can't fly, so he agrees to a road trip with his ditzy neighbor, Tara Duvall. She's shaking the Montana dust from her boots and leaving it all behind for a new start on Florida's sunny beaches. It's one speed bump after another as they deal with clashing personalities and frustrating obstacles, until romantic pit stops and minor mishaps suddenly start to look a whole lot like destiny.

#738 A SEAL'S SEDUCTION • *Uniformly Hot!*
by Tawny Weber

Admiral's daughter Alexia Pierce had no intention of ever letting another military man in her life, even if he was hot! But that was before she met Blake—and learned all the things a navy SEAL was good for....

REQUEST YOUR FREE BOOKS!
2 FREE NOVELS PLUS 2 FREE GIFTS!

HARLEQUIN®

Blaze®

red-hot reads!

YES! Please send me 2 FREE Harlequin® Blaze™ novels and my 2 FREE gifts (gifts are worth about $10). After receiving them, if I don't wish to receive any more books, I can return the shipping statement marked "cancel." If I don't cancel, I will receive 6 brand-new novels every month and be billed just $4.49 per book in the U.S. or $4.96 per book in Canada. That's a savings of at least 14% off the cover price. It's quite a bargain. Shipping and handling is just 50¢ per book in the U.S. and 75¢ per book in Canada.* I understand that accepting the 2 free books and gifts places me under no obligation to buy anything. I can always return a shipment and cancel at any time. Even if I never buy another book, the two free books and gifts are mine to keep forever.

151/351 HDN FVPV

Name _____ (PLEASE PRINT) _____

Address _____ Apt. #

City _____ State/Prov. _____ Zip/Postal Code

Signature (if under 18, a parent or guardian must sign)

Mail to the **Harlequin® Reader Service:**
IN U.S.A.: P.O. Box 1867, Buffalo, NY 14240-1867
IN CANADA: P.O. Box 609, Fort Erie, Ontario L2A 5X3

Want to try two free books from another line?
Call 1-800-873-8635 or visit www.ReaderService.com.

* Terms and prices subject to change without notice. Prices do not include applicable taxes. Sales tax applicable in N.Y. Canadian residents will be charged applicable taxes. Offer not valid in Quebec. This offer is limited to one order per household. Not valid for current subscribers to Harlequin Blaze books. All orders subject to credit approval. Credit or debit balances in a customer's account(s) may be offset by any other outstanding balance owed by or to the customer. Please allow 4 to 6 weeks for delivery. Offer available while quantities last.

Your Privacy—The Harlequin® Reader Service is committed to protecting your privacy. Our Privacy Policy is available online at www.ReaderService.com or upon request from the Harlequin Reader Service.

We make a portion of our mailing list available to reputable third parties that offer products we believe may interest you. If you prefer that we not exchange your name with third parties, or if you wish to clarify or modify your communication preferences, please visit us at www.ReaderService.com/consumerchoice or write to us at Harlequin Reader Service Preference Service, P.O. Box 9062, Buffalo, NY 14269. Include your complete name and address.

HBI3

Evangeline is surprised when her past lover turns out to be her fiancé's brother. How will she manage the one she loved and the one she has made a deal with?

Follow her path to love January 22, 2013, with

THE ONE THAT GOT AWAY

by Kelly Hunter

"The trouble with memories like ours," he said roughly, "is that you think you've buried them, dealt with them, right up until they reach up and rip out your throat."

Some memories were like that. But not all. Sometimes memories could be finessed into something slightly more palatable.

"Maybe we could try replacing the bad with something a little less intense," she suggested tentatively. "You could try treating me as your future sister-in-law. We could do polite and civil. We could come to like it that way."

"Watching you hang off my brother's arm doesn't make me feel civilized, Evangeline. It makes me want to break things."

Ah.

"Call off the engagement." He wasn't looking at her. And it wasn't a request. "Turn this mess around."

"We need Max's trust fund money."

"I'll cover Max for the money. I'll buy you out."

"What?" Anger slid through her, hot and biting. She could feel her composure slipping away but there was nothing else for it. Not in the face of the hot mess that was Logan. "No," she said as steadily as she could. "No one's buying me out of anything, least of all MEP. That company is *mine,* just as much as it is Max's. I've put six years into it, eighty-hour weeks of blood, sweat, tears and fears into making it the success it is. Prepping it for bigger opportunities, and one of those opportunities is just around the corner. Why on earth would I let you buy me out?"

He meant to use his big body to intimidate her. Closer, and closer still, until the jacket of his suit brushed the silk of her dress, but he didn't touch her, just let the heat build. His lips had that hard sensual curve about them that had haunted her dreams for years. She couldn't stop staring at them.

She needed to stop staring at them.

"You can't be in my life, Lena. Not even on the periphery. I discovered that the hard way ten years ago. So either you leave willingly…or I make you leave."

Find out what Evangeline decides to do by picking up THE ONE THAT GOT AWAY by Kelly Hunter. Available January 22, 2013, wherever Harlequin books are sold.